WARRIOR OF MY OWN

DIANA KNIGHTLEY

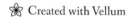

For Kevin, more and more and more...

CHAPTER 1

This is what I saw, Magnus standing in the kitchen holding a baby in his arms. His smile was wide. Emma was beaming. Chef Zach was cooking. I enjoyed the scene, domesticated and cheerful. Like a home. With Magnus as the center of attention.

Magnus held that baby like he loved to hold babies. That was one of the things about loving him — it slammed into me all at once but also in pieces as time went by. A Big Bang Theory of bursting hot love with meteorites of love pummeling me after. I guess it was a little like what he was telling me this morning in the shower. He loved me already, really loved me, but when I trusted him enough to run, he really loved me more.

That's how I felt all the time — more and more and more.

"So you've met Ben?"

"I have met him. He is a verra braw wee bairn who will become a strong warrior."

Emma's eyes went wide. "Right now we just want a happy baby, no warriors."

Magnus smiled. "He is a braw bairn." He nuzzled his face to

the baby's cheek. Ben smiled at him. "Nae a warrior, a chef like his dad."

Magnus passed the baby back to Emma and asked me, "Where is Madame Barbara?"

"She's upstairs, in her room. I'll go up and rouse her for breakfast. Back in a moment."

~

Ten minutes later I held Grandma's hand leading her into the room. "Hey Grandma, I have someone here who wants to see you. It's Magnus—"

My grandma looked up, directly at Magnus, and said, "Magnus Campbell? Why you haven't changed a bit!"

He swept her up in a bearhug then dropped her to her feet. "Madame Barb, tis good tae see ye again."

She looked up at him with a hand on each cheek staring into his eyes. "It's like no time has passed at all."

He said, "Twenty-five years has passed, but also, no time at all, because I'm a time-journeyer, Madame Barb. I jump around through time. That's why ye remember me verra well."

"Ah, now see, there's a magic to it. I should have known. And you've married my Katie?"

"I have, even before I met you. We were already family when I came tae live with ye in Maine."

"It makes perfect sense."

I laughed. "Grandma, a second ago I had to remind you where you are and now you're accepting Magnus's time travel story as a fact, easy as that?"

Grandma sat down, and Zach delivered a plate of waffles in front of her. "History is a circle, my dear, and memories have holes. Did you know Stephen Hawking died on the 300th anniversary of Galileo's birth? Also, that there are numbskulls in this world who believe the world is flat? So yes, time travel through worm holes in space, entanglements in each other's lives. It makes perfect sense, and forgetting things we already know is ludicrous, yet it happens. The world is a mystery and many times magic is the only explanation." It was a beautiful sentiment, and I found myself so excited whenever she said things like this — wise or funny or weird. Because moments later her mind would wander away and the lucid moment would be gone.

Magnus laughed outright. "Worm holes in space is an excellent metaphor, Madame Barb. I missed listening to you and Jack all those long nights in Maine talkin' about the mysteries of the universe. You made me believe I could understand orbits and time and threads but I journeyed again and realized my understandin' was mistaken."

"You never did figure out the dates?" I asked.

"Nae. I just journeyed from place tae place with nae sense of it until I arrived here last night as if twas nae the hardest thing in the world."

Zach, with a flourish, presented a large stack of waffles in front of Magnus, at least eight. He poured maple syrup on it.

Magnus said, "Perfect!"

Zach held up a finger, "Wait," and spiraled whipped cream on top.

Magnus's face was hilarious. His eyes so big I thought he might have an excitement stroke right there. He ate, shoveling big bites, smiling, and moaning happily.

I continued from our earlier conversation. "Except in Los Angeles, you came there right on time."

"I dinna, I arrived four days early."

"What did you do?"

"I lived on the side of the river in a camp."

"Oh my god, Magnus, you lived in a homeless camp in Los Angeles?"

He nodded.

"You looked so fresh when you entered the club!"

"I kept m'clothes in a backpack and changed intae them just afore I saw ye there."

"Wow, that's impressive. You've seen a side of Los Angeles I've never seen before."

"Aye." His eyes rested on Barb. She was staring into space, fidgeting with her food. "How are ye, Madame Barb?"

She said, "Do you know when Jack will be back? He's been gone overlong..."

Magnus nodded and turned a sad smile in my direction.

"Grandma, do you need Chef Zach to make you anything else?"

"No dear, tell Katie I went back to my room." She stood from the table and looked around confused. I started to stand but Magnus beat me to it.

"Madame Barb, tis me, Magnus Campbell, I will walk ye tae your room tae rest."

"Ah, Magnus, that is very good, I love it when you say 'ye,' but I bet all the girls tell you that."

"The only girl that matters is your granddaughter, Kaitlyn, and I think tis how I won her." He offered my grandma his arm and walked her upstairs to her room.

As soon as they left Emma said, "Are you so happy to have him home Katie?"

"I am, I can't believe it."

Quentin walked in just then. "Magnus is up?"

"You helped him up the boardwalk last night?"

"Yeah, he was a wreck."

He stood in the kitchen watching over Zach's shoulder, and then he picked a blueberry out of a bowl and tossed it in his mouth. "Traveling from 1492 must be cray-cray."

I rolled my eyes. "1702, I keep telling you this."

Quentin said, "Now I'm court-ordered, quit drinking, it makes it harder to understand. Whatever — medieval times."

Zach said, "You're off the date by *centuries*."

Quentin said, "Don't matter. When I hear history stuff I think dinosaurs, pirates, blah blah blah, and World War Two. Basically only the important stuff." Magnus came down the steps. "Right boss?"

"You are perfectly right, Master Quentin. My friends the deanosewers are truly noble creatures."

We all laughed. "How do you know about dinosaurs, Magnus? Most discoveries are... Wait, let me add the Natural History Museum to the list." I jumped up and got my list and sat at the dining room table, a new warm cup of coffee in front of me, jotting 'NHM, NY,' under 'the zoo,' and 'Disney World.'

Emma was sitting at one of the barstools, the baby settled nursing under her shirt. "I love that you guys accept this whole time-jumping thing as totally normal."

Quentin said, "Either I can work for a crazy man in a skirt with no idea how to work a car, or I can work for a superhero, costume-wearing, time-jumping, magic guy. I vote for the latter. Way cooler."

"Thank ye Quentin, I haena any idea what a superhero is but I like the sound of it." Magnus asked for another plate of waffles.

Quentin said, "Add the movie Thor to your list, Katie."

Magnus asked, "Madame Emma, you daena believe me about the time-journeys?"

She said, "I mean I do, I guess, it's the only way to explain it, but still... It can't be true. That doesn't happen. You can't just jump through time. But I have seen you disappear and reappear months later. I don't know, I don't believe in magic; I believe in God. I don't know how to explain it."

Magnus nodded thoughtfully. "I daena ken either, Madame Emma. I have the feeling I have gone against natural law and wonder what will happen tae my eternal soul. What price will I be expected tae pay?"

"Oh, Magnus, I didn't mean it like that. I wasn't—"

"Tis okay, I daena mind ye saying it. I am of the same opinion. I dinna ask tae do it, but I have done it now, many times. I pray asking forgiveness every day."

"Maybe you've been chosen?"

"Tis nae God's handiwork. Feels mighty devilish."

I decided to change the subject and asked, "While we have you all here, I wanted to remind you not to speak of this outside our household."

Quentin said, "Definitely not. No one can. As a matter of fact, as head of security, I think you should ask for non-disclosure agreements from everyone you've discussed it with so far."

"So far, outside of this group, it's only Hayley, and she told me to be quiet about it. So I think she's safe. But I'll get some printed in the morning. And speaking of things to do... What about going on a trip, Magnus?" I looked at the list in front of me. "We could drive south, stop at Kennedy Space Center, and drive all the way down to the Keys..."

Magnus's face drew down in a frown. He shook his head back and forth sadly.

"Why are you looking at me like that?"

He took a deep steadying breath.

"Seriously Magnus, why are you — you aren't — you can't — are you leaving again? What are you...?"

He continued to look at me quietly.

"No, you aren't. You can't."

He reached in his pocket and pulled out a ring with some very old iron keys and placed it on the table between us.

"What is that? Magnus, no. You put that away and don't you even..."

Emma watched me quietly. Chef Zach was looking from me to Magnus. Quentin stared at his coffee mug.

"I must away again."

I watched him for a moment. I was about to start screaming or maybe leap across the table, like with Braden, like a full-blown Banshee.

But I somehow held myself together. "Can everyone leave us alone for a moment?"

Quentin looked down at his watch. "I'm leaving, shift's done. Ted is outside Boss. I'll be back tonight at seven."

"Aye, Master Quentin, I will see ye tonight. Come early if ye need food first."

Chef Zach deposited some plates into the sink and asked Emma, "Want to take Ben for a walk on the beach?"

"I'm in my pajamas and yes." They stood and Emma put the baby in a sling and they went out the sliding doors to the deck.

This entire time Magnus watched me and I tried to look anywhere else.

My husband was leaving me again, and I literally just got him back, and yes, I was about to cry. I didn't remember signing on for this, loneliness hadn't been my plan. "Explain it to me."

"When I left Talsworth I had just killed the two guards. I couldna stay tae find Sean. On Lord Delapointe's desk there was a vessel and also the ring of keys to the prison cells. I stole them both. If I can return tae the castle, I could steal in with this key and get tae Sean in the prison. Free him and—"

I took a big gulp of coffee. "How would you get back to the right time? You haven't figured out timing, only location. You don't even know if—"

"When I return tae Scotland, the timing has been consistent. Only hours have passed, at most days. Without fail. Tis why I am confused by the mechanics."

"Since you left you've been in Los Angeles, in Maine, here in Florida, months have passed since I came back without you."

"'Tis true. I canna explain it. In Scotland my time has been a straight slow line. Here tis faster. I canna control it. But when I go tae Scotland, my time is nae different." He looked down at his napkin and adjusted its placement on the table. "But it daena matter how much time will pass. Tis all I know that I must go back. Sean is my brother. I must return and free him, or if tis too late I must ride with the Earl's army against Lord Delapointe."

"Wait, he's not dead?"

"Nae, you knocked him senseless but he is nae dead. I must return tae make it so."

I dropped my forehead to the table and rested it there on the cool wood. And then I spoke while my face was pressed to the surface. "You just came home."

"Aye."

I raised up and pushed the hair off my face. "I do not like being alone. And I really want to give you an ultimatum, but I won't because I honestly believe you would go anyway, that you would pick this instead of me. So I won't force it because I can't bear to watch you choose it over me."

His brow drew down. "I found ye first."

"I guess you did but it still feels a lot like being a second thought."

"I had the key tae save Sean in my sporran, and all I could think of was getting home tae ye. If he died, I may never forgive myself."

I blew out a breath of air. We were across the table from each other in a face off. I leaned out my hand and he took it beside his plate.

"I will always choose ye, Kaitlyn."

"Yes, I know. I'm sorry about what I said. So when?"

"I would need tae leave three days on."

I nodded slowly. "So I guess going to Disney World is out of the question."

"I haena any idea what ye are talking of, but aye, tis nae possible. I will come home though and this time I will have this whole tragedy finished so I may bide."

"Okay. Yeah. Okay." I looked sadly down at my arms stretched across the table meeting him halfway. "Want a party? The gang would probably like to see you. That way I can prove you aren't a figment of my imagination."

"I would like a party. An ice cream party. Chef Zach promised me we could make it in a machine."

"Perfect."

He jumped from his seat. "Stay right there. I want tae talk tae ye about the numbers."

He disappeared into our bedroom and returned a moment later with his sporran and dropped it with a thud to the table. He opened it and pulled out the vessel and sat in a chair beside me.

He twisted the vessel and strange markings glowed in a ring around the middle. Magnus aligned a few of the markings and the vessel hummed and vibrated.

He gently rolled it to the table.

"I didn't notice it do that before."

"Twas quite shocking when it came tae life. Lady Mairead haena fully explained the workings, I had tae discover it for myself."

We investigated it without touching because there was no need for an unnecessary time jump. "What do the markings mean?"

"I daena ken the purpose. But I found some similarities tae the numbers I recite when I jump."

He gingerly tapped the middle ring. Then twisted and turned it. "See the markings here? Tis a number. And this blank spot? I have guessed at its purpose. I canna ken their meanin', but I have gotten closer tae the pattern."

"It's a lot like you know more and understand less."

"Much like it. Studyin' with your grandpa Jack I learned tae use longitude and latitude and with an equation I can go to exact locations, tis a help."

He added, "If I jump, daena grab my arm."

I nodded solemnly.

He pushed at one of the rings so the markings shifted.

I asked, "Does the ring turn easily?"

"Tis verra easy until the vessel grabs ye."

He tapped the ring and the markings shifted again. "I was wonderin' if ye would be able tae make sense of it."

I read the markings and came up with nothing. "We need an expert, but I don't know who. Neil deGrasse Tyson? Bill Nye? Elon Musk? I don't know who it would be."

Magnus explained how he came up with the numbers and then how he tried the different numbers to see which would work.

"You jumped each time for the science of it?"

"To see if the numbers were true."

"So the science."

"Aye, if tis the word, then that is what I did."

"Have you figured out how to make it not hurt so badly?"

"I have not. But if I prepare for the trip, the right clothing, some food in my sporran, tis nae so bad."

"I'll help you pack then."

I started another list:

Food.

Medicine.

Weapons.

Clothing.

"This time you should take a horse."

CHAPTER 2

*H*ayley, Michael, and James with his new girlfriend, Lee Anne, all came over after work. Hayley now called herself Aunt Hayley and commanded the room bossily, but seemed uninterested in Baby Ben generally. I had figured out pretty early on that Hayley was not interested in kids at all, but Michael was now going to be a school teacher; they were going to get married; he would probably be interested in having kids before long.

James introduced his girlfriend around as if we would be impressed. She was an interesting choice for him, beautiful, like a well-practiced Barbie with the brain-power of a hunk of plastic. She said, when we mentioned Quentin wouldn't be there until later, "Oh, that's right, he's your black friend," in her languid southern drawl, with a pretty sneer on her outlined lips.

I glanced at Hayley and she looked at me wide-eyed.

A moment later Hayley and I were standing in the kitchen. "Help me, Katie, she is a mind-numbed, hate-spouting idiot. What am I going to do?"

"I don't know, come here more often? Does James seem to like her?"

"I think he's totally in love."

"Ugh."

We met everyone on the back deck. Lee Anne was giggling at something Magnus said, flipping her hair, arching her back just a bit, super flirtatiously. James's brow was drawn down.

Served him right I supposed, since he was usually the center of flirtatious attention.

And of course Lee Anne was flirting with Magnus. He looked amazing wearing his modern jeans and shirt. They had been laundered and folded and waiting for him for months and months.

When I walked out on the deck, he raised his eyes to mine and for a moment time stood still.

It was a moment where my mind said breathlessly — *yes.*

And I swore I could hear him say inside my head, deep and resonating — *aye.*

Hayley said as she passed through the sliding door, "Jesus Christ girl, that is some serious smolder."

Emma was in a rocking chair on the deck nursing Baby Ben. Zach had a table set up with an whirring ice cream maker. He was assembling bowls of toppings and sauces, setting up a regular ice cream shop in Magnus's honor.

James said, "I brought you a present Boss."

Magnus laughed, "Last I checked I wasna your boss, Master Cook. Has something changed in our friendship?"

"Katie bought some apartments over on First Avenue. I'm the contractor."

Magnus smiled at me. "You have become lord of the land, my Kaitlyn?"

I laughed. "I might be the landlord of a tiny plot, yes."

Magnus shrugged at James. "Sounds like Kaitlyn is your boss."

"Yeah, well, true," James chuckled. "I brought a present for you both then. I'll get it from the truck."

James disappeared downstairs and returned a few minutes later with his tool belt and a box with Tiki Toss printed across it. He placed the box in front of Magnus. "You have the perfect deck for this." He set about installing the game at the other end.

The goal of the game was to aim a ring for a hook on a surfboard shape. Magnus asked, "We toss this tiny ring? How will the women see our muscles?"

I laughed, "Depends on how you pose as you toss it."

A few more people showed up then and soon enough the ice cream was ready. Vanilla, though Zach had about eight more ready-made flavors to choose from.

Magnus was appropriately mystified and impressed by the ice cream machine and the wide variety of toppings. He sprinkled so many colored sprinkles on his bowl that it was impossible to see the ice cream, assuring us that, "Highlanders love these tiny candy bits." Then he happily took a bite, made a face, and added, "'Tis nae my favorite."

Chef Zach cracked up. "I told you that was too much."

Magnus shook his head forlornly. "I have ruined the majestic display."

Chef Zach took Magnus's bowl to the kitchen to scrape sprinkles from it and returned a moment later with just the vanilla in a bowl.

Magnus said, "'Tis just how Highlanders like their ice cream."

And everyone laughed.

We had ice cream sundaes, played Tiki Toss, drank a lot of beer, and ate grilled cheese sandwiches that Zach whipped up for us. It was beautiful weather. We enjoyed friends and fun with a late sunset and an afternoon that went on and on. It was a wonderful evening. I tried very hard not to think about Magnus leaving because what would be the point — to be sad while he was here?

The truth was our time together was fleeting, had always been. Like all time ours was a mystery of interwoven strands moving together, sometimes going alone. I had to make sure that our time together was good. Even if it was short.

Especially if it was short.

But that was also a lot of pressure to always be smiling.

A look passed between us again — *yes* — *aye.*

Night came on, the sky had grown dark. We were sitting at tables, watching the game, candles flickering, drinking, and laughing.

Hayley said, "Now that you're back Magnus is Katie going to take you to Orlando like she's been dreaming about?"

We were sitting beside each other, leaned back in deck chairs. Magnus finished the beer in his hand. "Sadly I must go away again."

Hayley said, "What? What are you talking about? When?"

"Three days hence."

Hayley, like a good friend, turned to me with a frown. "Oh no, he's leaving again?"

I nodded.

Hayley protested, "It's not fair Magnus. It's not fair to Katie. Can't you figure something out?"

"I have pressing business—"

"Get someone else to do it."

I said, "Hayley, he's the boss. You know what that's like. He's the only one who can do it."

She said, "I'm the boss of like a ton of people and I can take a day. It's not that freaking hard, you just have to prioritize what's important."

"Hayley, it's not like that."

"It's exactly like that." She turned to Magnus, "If you sir, gave one thought to Katie you wouldn't be leaving again."

Michael said, "Whoa now, babe."

"It's true, she's been heartbroken all year. How many days have you been together since your marriage?"

I said, "Like a week."

Lee Anne said, "Oh, are you in the Navy? My sister's husband is in the—"

James said, "Nah, it's not like that, he's just got work."

I pointed at Lee Anne, "But yeah, like a Navy wife. Lots of wives have to deal with this…"

Hayley said, "You know it's not the same. I'm just saying Magnus shouldn't put you through it again."

Magnus said, "I wish I dinna have tae, but I do."

Hayley took a deep breath. "How are you going to deal with it Katie?"

"I don't know, I'm trying to be a grown up about it."

Hayley rolled her eyes and huffed.

I decided to try to lighten the mood by being over-dramatic and collapsed on the table. "Oh! If I had only known getting married would mean growing up! I didn't realize it was going to be so tragic and lonely."

Hayley looked at Michael. "If we get married are you going to leave me?"

Michael looked from me to Magnus to Hayley. "Um, not sure what to say, but no. I'm gonna take classes at college, then get a job."

Hayley gestured at Michael. "See? Marriage isn't supposed to be lonely. It's supposed to be waking up every day making each other crazy."

Magnus was watching my face, looking at Hayley's and back to mine. "I warned ye. I said twould be hard tae marry me."

I grinned, still trying to lighten the mood though my heart

didn't feel light at all. "You, my love, did warn me but this is what I heard... jaw line, sexy, blah blah blah, shoulders, hot, dangerous, biceps bulging, yum, kilt, and sexy. It was very hard to hear you over your hotness."

His brow drew down with his familiar look of confusion. He asked, his voice low and rumbling, "Do ye regret marrying me?"

"Never. Not once. No."

He took my hand and stroked the back of it.

Hayley raised a brow. "Not once? How about when Lady Mairead put a knife to your throat—"

I shot her a shut up look but it was too late.

Magnus dropped his voice. "What did — Lady Mairead — when?"

I realized that James and everyone was looking at us, listening. "Hayley's joking. Lady Mairead and I got into a thing. She's joking about the knife." I turned to Magnus. "I didn't want to worry you. Let's talk about it—"

Magnus leaned forward in his seat. "I need tae know Kaitlyn. What did Lady Mairead do?"

Quietly I answered, "She just — when I returned from Scotland and came home, Lady Mairead was waiting for me. She was furious. Accused me of letting you leave against her orders. She told me I would never see you again."

Hayley said, "Actually if you think about it she made you think he was dead."

"Hayley, you are not helping."

She rocked her head back and forth, her words a little slurring. "I'm not hurting either, gotta tell the truth. Even if it is about someone's bitchy mom."

James said, "You didn't tell me about that."

"It's not your business — mine, Magnus's." I directed my attention back to Magnus.

"Except you dinna tell me."

"I would have... It just didn't seem important enough to say it right away."

"What else did she say?"

I pulled toward him and spoke so that only he could hear. "She pulled a knife on me. Told me she wanted to kill me, but she would let me live. I just wouldn't ever see you again."

"How long ago was this?"

"Months ago."

He pulled me by both hands toward his waist, wrapped my arms around his chest all but pulling me from my chair, and kissed me on top of my head. "I am sorry I have brought danger tae ye, mo reul-iuil." He spoke it quietly into my hair.

It made me a little misty-eyed. It had been a long bleak time, but it was nice he knew about it and was sorry for it. I nodded my head against his chest.

Hayley said, "Aw, now see, that is so sweet. Okay Magnus, I forgive you. Because you are so romantic to my Katie. Forget I said anything."

"Madame Hayley, you have been a good friend to Kaitlyn Campbell and me this day."

"Good!" She hiccuped and seemed to have lost interest in the conversation.

The party continued for a while longer, Magnus and James had a Tiki Toss battle to the end and we all cheered for one or the other. They were preening and posing like two Olympic athletes as they tossed the tiny ring. It was comical and lifted our mood, yet between the laughs Magnus's face clouded over. He became thoughtful and ruminating before he would shake himself out of it and laugh again a moment later.

I decided he must be thinking about his mission in a few days. I had my own mission. Tomorrow we would be moving my grandmother into her assisted-living home. I needed to concentrate on that.

CHAPTER 3

Finally, people began to go home. Emma disappeared with the baby up to her room. Chef Zach cleaned the whole kitchen, offered everyone a last round of beers, left some extras in a tub of ice, and followed her upstairs. Having a live-in party staff was awesome. Hayley was the last to leave. She hugged Magnus extra long and gave a long slurring speech about how he was her "Favorite of Kaitlyn's husbands" and "Don't let all that garbage Michael was saying earlier hurt your feelings. Michael doesn't understand true love, because Michael is a poop head."

Michael helped her down to their Uber leaving me and Magnus at the teak table alone on the deck. It was a beautiful night, stars above, the sound of the ocean reaching our ears because the music ended and now it was quiet — crashing waves, rustling sea grass. The gentle hum of the air conditioning.

Magnus leaned back in his chair and looked down at his hands.

"You okay?"

He took another deep breath.

"Don't let what Hayley was saying bother you too much. She was just drunk. Plus she doesn't have any room to talk. She and Michael don't have a good relationship by any standard."

"'Tis nae the words of Mistress Hayley, nae really. I canna stop thinking of ye with Lady Mairead's knife point at your throat."

"Yeah, well...she is — you know, you say not to trust her. Let's just say her threats can't be trusted either."

"I believe her threats are the one thing she is verra truthful about. She knows how much ye mean tae me, I am surprised at her actions."

I looked at him sadly for a few moments then said, "Would you like to do something cool? Something super fun that will get your mind off of all of this? Because mothers and their crazy, *idle* threats are as common as fleas. We need to scratch it off and continue our lives."

He chuckled. "Och aye, mo reul-iuil, what is fun?"

"Skinny-dipping. It's the perfect night for it. Warm, languid waves, dark, a bit drunk out."

"Are we now? That does sound good."

"I'll race you." I shoved back my chair, jumped from my seat and bounded down the boardwalk, giggling loudly, actually more like a squealing with Magnus in full chase behind. Clomp clomp clomp. I skipped down the steps jumped to the sand and sprinted across the dunes. The tide was low, the waves non-existent. I whipped my shirt off over my head, unclasped my bra, and tossed them both over my shoulder. I unbuttoned my shorts and dropped them to the side with a kick, and then just before my feet hit the water, I slipped my panties off, wiggled my hips, and tossed them way far behind me. I splashed into the warm water until it was thigh deep and then dropped all the way in. I came up a minute later and looked back at the beach.

Magnus was hopping on one leg trying to pull a shoe off while laughing.

"God, you are so slow!"

He got a shoe off and tossed it up the beach and then balanced on the other foot, pulled off the second shoe and tossed that up the beach too. Then he pulled his shirt up over his head, all muscle-bound arms and shoulders and then, oh abs, and — his pants hit the ground and he bounded in after me doing a half dive and coming up just in front of me with a "phwesha!"

"Hi."

"Hello Madame Kaitlyn." He chuckled. Two strong hands grabbed my ass and pulled me close. A small wave picked us up, rolled under us, and dropped us down. My calves slithered against his skin, soft kicks and gentle brushes. "You are verra slippery."

I grinned and slid my arms around his neck. "Lotion." I ran my hands down his back, still not used to the crisscrossing scars there, but not minding them because they were a part of him now. "How come we haven't done this before?"

"'Tis my first time all the way in the ocean."

"It is? Really? It is? I mean, I guess so, but — wow. Well, my love, this is the Atlantic Ocean and..."

One of his hands flitted and played between my legs and his fingers explored and I lost track of my words as his lips went over mine, his tongue playing deep in my mouth. "And?" he asked as he pushed inside my body.

I moaned happily, wrapping my legs around his waist, inviting him in closer, more, "It's salty and — oh god, Magnus—" The feel of his hands clasping me tight to his body was amazing. I arched back, floating on the surface of the water, concentrated power and relaxed motion inside me. The sky was flung with stars, deep black, the water shimmering, and my husband, head bowed, eyes closed, intense. His hands holding me so strong and sure, pulling me in, pushing me away, return and release. I rose up to wrap my arms around him again and floated just above. My tongue pressed to the salt of his neck, moaning into his skin, repeating my mantra, *ohgodohgodohgod,* as his body rushed full of force and power. And that now familiar feeling of Magnus, finishing, still and driven, hot and filling and pulsing and deep-breath-exhaling — *aaahhh* — more felt than said.

And then a long delicious pause. Where slowly mind returned and memory and place and touch slowly bit by bit, until consciousness was full again. Oh. It was me, Magnus, love. My lips felt his pulse. His body held a hum. The water was warm and lifted me away and dropped me back on him.

God, I loved him. His temple was pressed to my cheek. The salt of his sweat mingled with ocean and breeze. "How do you like it?"

"Tis verra fun."

"We should add surfing to our list—"

Suddenly from the direction of the house, faint, Quentin's voice, "Boss!" He was running closer down the sand. "Magnus, Kaitlyn, something's—" He got to the water's edge out of breath. "Barb is freaking out."

"Oh crap," I plowed to shore.

Magnus said, "Quentin, we arna clothed, can ye turn around?"

Quentin turned quickly away. "Yes Boss, sorry."

I scurried past his turned back and scooped up my panties and my shirt, having forgotten any kind of towel. I pulled them on my dripping skin, tugging the shorts up as I ran. Stuffing my bra in my back pocket as I raced up the steps and down the boardwalk to the house. Every single light was on and now I could hear it, the baby crying, and something else — shrieking.

"Oh no no no no."

When I arrived at the sliding door, Emma was consoling an

inconsolable baby in the kitchen while my grandma was in the middle of the living room banging her hands to her ears. Her expression full-blown traumatized.

"Grandma?" I walked up timidly, and rightly so. As I approached, she began to swing wildly. Her screeches filled the house. "Grandma? Barb? It's me Kaitlyn." I tried to catch her arms to hold them firm but her body seemed frail and breakable and lost. But also she was frightened and lashing out. I ducked as she swung at my head. "It's me, Katie, your granddaughter!"

She shrieked again.

Magnus came in behind me.

Zach and Emma were huddled, bouncing the baby, shhhh-shhhhhhhhing.

"Grandma! Barb!" I got her arms pinned to her sides, my arms wrapped around her body. "Barb! It's me Katie! I'll call your son, John. You want to talk to Johnny?"

She shrieked, her mouth so close to my ear and so shrill I worried about my eardrum.

"Barb, you take it easy. It's all good. It's me Katie. This is your house. This is the baby. You know, Baby Ben. You love Baby Ben. He's just crying right now, shhhhhhhh shhhhhhhhhh." I ran my hands down her hair, repeating, cajoling, "Please Grandma Barb, shhhhhh, shhhhhhhh." I calmed her down enough to lead her to the stairs. "We're going to go back to your room, shhhhh, shhhhhh—"

"Where's Jack?"

"Jack isn't here Grandma. He's in heaven now—"

"Is that Baby Ben crying?"

Relief washed over me. She was coming back. "Yes, Baby Ben is crying, but it's okay. The baby is okay. You're okay."

We walked up the stairs, my arms holding her tightly.

"Did I scare the baby? I'm sorry I scared the baby."

"Oh no Grandma, you didn't scare the baby. You were crying

along with the baby. That's fine. We all want to sometimes. Cause just between us that baby has some strong lungs. He can really scream if he wants and so it's okay." I pushed her door open and helped her on the bed. "If you want to scream too, it's okay. Do you need to go to the bathroom?"

"No honey, I'm okay now." I pulled the comforter over her.

Magnus lightly knocked. "I brought a glass of water." He brought it to the bedside table.

Grandma said, "It's so sweet Magnus, thank you." She patted him on the cheek and rolled over on her side.

"Goodnight Grandma."

She nodded her head on the pillow.

I stood and watched her for a moment before I tiptoed out of the room.

Magnus followed me downstairs. The baby had stopped crying and was nursing in Emma's arms on the couch. Emma looked exhausted. Her head lolled back on the cushions. Zach was perched on the arm's edge. As soon as he saw me he said, "I'm so sorry Katie, that was — I'm so—"

"Zach, you don't have to apologize. What on earth would you apologize for?"

He glanced at the stairs.

I said, "Because Barb's got some screws loose and rattling around upstairs, you do not need to apologize."

"But the baby—"

"The baby gets to scream and holler. Baby Ben gets to cry. Do you live here?"

"I do."

"Yes you do. You're like a brother to Magnus, plus you feed him. Don't you feed Barb too?"

He nodded.

"You're the goddamned glue holding this house together. We would literally starve without you. And look at Emma here, she made a whole person. She's feeding a whole person. She keeps my bathroom stocked with toilet paper, and I would die without her, and I'm not being over-dramatic. You don't apologize for the baby. Baby Ben gets to scream. And you know what, I was going to apologize for Barb, but the thing is, Barb gets to scream. Everyone gets to scream if the shitstorm gets too rough. So there you go. Screaming is allowed." I finished, my hands on my hips, breathing heavy.

Zach smiled. "You don't want us to move?"

"God no. I mean, if you hate it here. If it doesn't work for you, but I really really really need you and like you living here. You know what Magnus does when the baby is crying?" I gestured toward Magnus. "He sighs and smiles. I don't know what weird happiness that is, but he likes it."

Magnus said, "Reminds me of home. Tis always a wee bairn with a cry full of noise."

I pointed to Magnus with a, "See?"

Zach said, "I don't want it to feel like it's either-or. She's your grandma..."

"She is. I love her. But the nursing home has an opening. She moves there tomorrow, and it's not your fault. It's because that's been the plan. I love her desperately. I didn't want her to live in Maine, so far away, but down the street with round-the-clock care. This is not a terrible thing." I stared at the ground for a moment. "We can make it work..."

Everyone nodded. I went and sat on the arm of the couch near Emma and the baby. "I am truly sorry about the drama."

"I know, I'm sorry about the screaming."

I shook my head and stroked the cheek of tiny Ben, now sleeping peacefully. I whispered, "I'm sorry Barb interrupted your perfectly epic solitary scream session, I know you like center stage."

Emma giggled. Zach stood and stretched. "It's one a.m. Magnus, need something from the kitchen?"

Magnus grinned. "Do ye have more ice cream?"

He followed Zach to the kitchen and I took a deep breath, went to the linen closet for towels to finally dry my hair, and followed them.

CHAPTER 4

I brushed my teeth staring at myself in the mirror a little buzzed still, a little satiated from the bowl of ice cream but also jangled. My husband was leaving. My grandma was wearing heavy on my heart. This shit was hard, so freaking hard. How did I go from carefree to so deep in — it sucked.

Magnus stepped into the room, "Kaitlyn?" I was standing at the sink staring at the faucet. He pulled me into a hug and without even knowing it was about to happen I sobbed into his chest. He held me tight, stroking down the back of my hair. He led me down the hallway to the bed and sat me down on it and kneeled in front of me. "You are all right?"

I shook my head. "It's just so hard. It's all so hard." I sobbed into my hands.

"Your grandmother daena remember ye."

"I know." I collapsed on his shoulder and cried into his neck.

"She remembers me, perhaps we could go back in time? We could introduce ye tae the Madam Barb of yore and she would know ye as you are now, clear as day."

I sat up, grabbed a tissue, and wiped my eyes. "No, thank you.

That's a very sweet idea, but it seems unfair to give her fake memories. Like I would be playing with her mind. I just need to focus on my own memories with her."

"Aye." He held my knees. "Tomorrow we move her to the new home?"

"Yep. I'm super conflicted and will probably cry a lot."

"Chef Zach and I will move boxes and ye and Ben will cry."

"And I'll be able to visit her every day."

"It will be quiet and comfortable and nae quite so heartbreaking. But if it daena work, we'll bring her back."

"It's a deal." I straightened my back and brushed the hair from my forehead. "Of course you won't be here, I'll be making that decision on my own."

He nodded quietly and stood.

He dropped his clothes off and I stood and dropped mine off to the floor and then we both climbed into the bed. First night climbing into bed together since he came home, not even twenty-four hours before. He put up an arm and I snuggled into his chest, kissing his skin closest to my lips, so tired from the excitement and drama of the day and it was late, very late and there was a whole lot to do tomorrow—

CHAPTER 5

We woke in the stillness of dawn and made love. Our room was full of grey light. Dark enough that I kept my eyes closed. His hand moved along my skin measuring, caressing, investigating. I writhed and wriggled with his massage, waking bit by bit to his touch, slowly, sleepily, quietly. It was too early to be awake but also, every minute was borrowed.

By the time his hand plunged between my thighs and pulled me toward him, my eyes opened onto the light of a barely there morning. I flung the covers back ready to be awake, fully. When I climbed on his body, he whispered in my ear, "Good morn."

I panted against his cheek and kissed the curl of hair just by his ear. "Good morning love."

We pushed and rocked against each other rising and falling. He said, "Speak it again."

"Good morning love of mine." My voice was breathless and gravelly, my lips wet, our kisses lingering.

"Tis good tae have your voice in my ear."

I pressed my hands to his wide chest and rose up to ride him into the full light of day.

~

We showered and dressed together emerging to a big breakfast and a bustling morning. Quentin stayed after his shift. Zach was ready to work. I packed boxes. Grandma puttered around helping. Magnus helped load. Quentin kind of bossed us around too much as everyone carried Grandma's things down the steps to the Mustang and Quentin's truck.

Grandma kept getting sidetracked with long stories as I wrapped objects and packed them into boxes. Magnus hung on her every word. He remembered a photo of my grandparents when they were married. And the two of them talked about my grandfather. I joined in but it was such a complicated thing. My grandpa was the guy who held my hand when I was five and we walked around the lake. He introduced me to my first hockey game. Most of my memories of him were the blurry and unformed memories of youth.

Magnus on the other hand went to a bar with my grandparents and laughed and joked with them around the dinner table. Grownup-people laughing. It was almost enough for me to imagine going back to meet them in 1995. But not quite enough. My grandma's mind was so confused it couldn't be a good thing to meet her before I was born.

We packed it all up and loaded it all. It was hot, sweaty work, but also a new first because I had never worked alongside my husband before. I liked it.

He laughed. He was in good spirits. He touched me or smiled in my direction when we passed. He was the only reason I was able to get through it because actually doing it sucked. I felt like a traitor, like I should have tried harder, maybe hired a nursing staff. Heck, I should have gotten a nursing degree then I could've taken care of Grandma around the clock. But also, I didn't. And she needed more care, specialized, for longer.

The staff met me at the front door and we moved Grandma into her room in no time at all. And so when Quentin left to go to his own apartment and Zach to go back to the house, Magnus and I stayed in her room. We went to the dining room with her to eat an early lunch and walked the grounds, all of us together. Until around twelve-thirty when she was exhausted and wanted a nap, and I finally took my leave. Hugging her goodbye I promised to visit her the following day. I held hands with Magnus, not speaking, down to the car and then, once in the driver's seat, I hunched over the steering wheel and dissolved into tears.

Magnus put his hand on my back and waited.

And then I drove us home.

CHAPTER 6

Quentin's truck was at the house.

Magnus said, "Tis nae his shift, why is he here?"

He rose from the car as Quentin opened the front door and rushed down the stairs.

"Magnus, we've had an issue, something—" His eyes flitted to me and he gestured for Magnus to follow him.

"Is it the baby, oh god, not the baby?" I asked from the car.

"No, not the baby."

I watched Magnus follow Quentin to the house, and I stayed in the car for a moment. Then I said to myself, "Quentin didn't tell me I had to stay in the car and who the hell is he, anyway? He's not the boss of me." I dropped the keys into my purse and ascended to the main floor. When I entered, Zach and Emma were standing in the kitchen. Baby Ben was in Emma's arms. Same as usual but they had worried expressions.

"Everything cool?"

Zach said, "Nah, somebody's been here."

My heart dropped. "While you were here alone Emma? Security was here though, right?"

She nodded. "He didn't see anything though and someone came in the house. Luckily I was upstairs with Ben. I heard it though, someone was here walking around inside the house."

"Crap."

I crossed the living room to where Magnus and Quentin stood on the deck looking up at the sky.

"What happened?"

"Someone has been in the house, Emma heard it."

"What did Ted see?"

Quentin answered, "Nothing, he didn't see anything, and Emma didn't have his phone number. He was out front near the road, and Emma was afraid to come out of her room."

"Well, that's a couple of security issues right there. It was probably a thief?"

Magnus shook his head.

"So what then?" But I had a guess.

Quentin said, "Let me take you up to the office, the safe has been opened."

We filed up the stairs. The safe door was wide open. The money and jewels were all there. The time travel device was still there. Magnus asked, "Why is there only one?"

"Lady Mairead took it the night she threatened me."

"You dinna mention that before." He scowled down at the contents of the safe.

"I was going to, we just keep getting interrupted."

Magnus shifted the contents investigating but I didn't need to look because on the desk was a glass bowl that hadn't been there before. It was from downstairs. The one that held Beach House-scented potpourri. The one I used to threaten Lady Mairead with when she broke in.

The potpourri was gone and what was left was... Ash. A pile of ash. A fire had been started inside a bowl inside my house. What had been burned? "Magnus is my contract with Lady Mairead still in the safe?"

"Nae tis gone." He stood to investigate the bowl. "Daena touch it, there may be poison about it." He walked around looking on the other tables and shelves.

A couple of the pieces of ash had a yellow edge from the legal pad. "She burnt the contract. That's what's in here. But where's the potpourri?" I asked.

The two men were looking around the room disinterested in my question because it was a rather insignificant question, really.

I wandered out of the room and down the stairs. "Zach, is the potpourri from the bowl in the trash can?"

He lifted the lid and shook his head.

I glanced around and then went to my bedroom. I don't know what made me do it. The bed was made. The room seemed like it was just as I left it, perhaps a little more fragrant than before. I went to the bed and pulled back the covers. Little flaky bits of smelly dried flowers were spread all over my nice sheets. I clapped my hand to my mouth. My heart dropped. I was terrified. It hit me in the gut — I was unsafe and about to be alone again.

A moment later Magnus stuck his head through the door. "Anythin'?" His eyes landed on the bed. He crossed the room and swept me up in his arms and held me strong and sure and long, but my mind was whirling around in a panic.

"I have tae..." Magnus voice trailed off.

I waited for what he was going to say, but then asked, "What are we going to do? She can come and go. She knows you're here. She's threatening me."

"Och, aye. She has miscalculated verra much if she thinks I will stand for this."

I nodded, released from his arms, and brushed my hair from my face. "I need to clean this up. I can't let Emma do it. She's a nursing mom. You think I should wear gloves?"

"Och aye, she is nae tae be—"

"You know, here, we call someone like this a stone-cold bitch. 'Not to be trusted' is like an employee that steals forty dollars out of a drawer. Someone walking around poisoning and threatening — that shit deserves a different description all together."

He nodded, "Aye, she deserves much more." He pushed a lock of hair off my cheek and tucked it behind my ear.

CHAPTER 7

*S*o while Magnus made apologies to the staff and promised he would tighten security and make everything so much better, I cleaned my room — in gloves. I wiped all the surfaces. I swept the potpourri into a trash bag. I put the sheets into the trash bag too. Emma and Zach and Ben went to the store to buy me new sheets.

I was exhausted. It had been a giant shitstorm of a day. It started with Grandma's meltdown in the middle of the night, waking to drop her off in a home away from my home, having some weird seventeenth century curse-threat on my life and now cleaning it up.

And then my husband came in to the room to tell me, hey, let's go out and run through some "exercises" because he was worried about how I was going to protect myself while he was gone, probably for months.

So yeah, I was not in a good head space.

But I took a deep breath and decided I would try to be a helpful partner in protecting myself. Plus I had taken a few kickboxing classes. I was tired but it crossed my mind that I might impress him.

I threw on my yoga pants and a cropped athletic bra looking great if I did say so myself. Also pretty capable.

We were out on the beach running through our drills. Magnus and I were sparring with knives and he was telling me to lunge.

I lunged.

He pushed me off and made me do it again and again and again.

Each time pushing me off and making me do it over.

I was trying to be upbeat. I was trying to try. I was happy to have him home and wanted to focus on that. But I was also one big piece of wrecked mood. There was too much going on in my head.

So I missed his cues that he was getting frustrated. That was my bad.

His bad was oh so much worse.

He made me lunge again and pushed me off. "Nae Kaitlyn, tis weak. You will die with a lunge like that."

"Not if I do this." I kicked weakly on his hip, wiggled my hips, and smiled flirtatiously.

"Stop smiling and lunge again."

I tried to look more serious and lunged again.

Magnus knocked my knife from my hand, grabbed my arm, twisted it behind my back, shoved me face first into the sand, and pulled my hair back.

I screamed.

He pressed on my back and growled in my ear. "You are dead."

Sand was in my mouth and nose. I tried to get my hands to my head. My hair was about to rip from my scalp. The pressure in my back hurt and his voice was terrifying.

A sob escaped me with a whimper. I begged, "Please, Magnus, please—"

He shoved himself off.

I clutched my head and curled up in the fetal position. I spit sand from my mouth. It was in my nose, all over my face. I tried to catch my jagged breaths — but I couldn't control them. My anger was rising, tamping down the fear from a second before. I was about to have a gigantic total melt down.

His breaths were heavy behind me, but I wasn't going to look at him — I might never, ever, ever look at him again.

I pushed myself up and stood and spit more sand. I swiped at the sand covering my face but it was wet and thick.

I turned to leave.

Magnus said, "We arna finished."

I refused to turn back. "We are too finished. We are totally finished."

I heard him heave himself up.

Beside me was a pile of knives on a duffel bag. Without thinking I dove for one and lunged screeching at my husband surprising him so much he lost his footing and fell to the ground. I held the knife just in front of his eyes, my hand shaking with anger. "How dare you? Are you a fucking monster? A barbarian? Is that what you are?"

His eyes wouldn't leave the knife point.

"Are you a fucking barbarian Magnus?"

"Nae."

My voice had gone all dark and deep. "You want to scare me? To teach me a lesson? I'm the motherfucking matriarch of this family. I've got people that depend on me, that I take care of. I run a fucking household, and you want to scare me, make me cry? Don't you ever."

My hand went weak, tears welled up, and my voice cracked. "Don't you make me scared of you Magnus, don't you do it." I dropped the knife to the side and collapsed on his chest. "It's not fair. I will hate you. Don't make me hate you, don't do that." His arms went around my body. "Don't make me scared of you, I don't want to be."

His lips pressed on my forehead and brought another sob to my chest.

I asked, "Why would you?"

He held me tight to his chest. "I daena ken." He pressed his cheek to my forehead and continued, "I wanted ye tae feel afraid as I am for ye."

"The reason I'm not as afraid is because I trust you and I love you and I know you'll take care of me. Why would you want to ruin that? Don't ruin it."

He bowed his head near mine. "I winna Kaitlyn, I winna."

I heard Quentin's approach and felt Magnus's hand wave him away. Magnus adjusted his position so I was encircled in his arms and then we just sat huddled together. I tried to gain control of my breaths, to stanch my tears, and gather my strength. I didn't know how I would get past this, but I knew I would need to. My best bet was to stay in his arms until it was comfortable again until I wanted to be there.

Even if it took all day.

So we sat in the sand, and maybe he was thinking the same thing — that he would keep me in between his legs and his arms until I was comfortable and not about to run away.

And we breathed together, his breath near my forehead. The scent of our sweat in my nose.

After a very long time I hiccuped.

And then quickly hiccuped again and giggled.

"Och aye," he said with a sigh of relief.

I hiccuped again.

He raised my chin with a gentle hand and brushed sand off my face. Then he reached for his shirt to the side and wadded it up and used it to brush my face more. "Close your eyes, tis in your lashes."

I hiccuped again and looked up at his face. "You scared the shit out of me, don't do that again."

He nodded. "I winna."

"Good." I hiccuped again.

A smile worked at the edge of his mouth. "The mother-fucking matriarch needs a glass of water."

I giggled. "Don't you forget it."

"I winna, Kaitlyn, you have my word."

"Good." I stood and offered him a hand to help him up. "And I trust you, see how much better that is?"

"Tis a great deal better, but ye are still shaking."

"Yeah, I'm really at the end of being able to (hiccup)—would you mind if I took a (hiccup) nap? I just..."

He walked me into the house and after a glass of water I went and curled up around my knees in bed thinking, "I don't have enough time with Magnus to be wasting it sleeping," and, "Does Lady Mairead really want me dead?" And, "I moved my grandma into a home this morning," and, "My husband came really close to breaking my heart today," and a moment later I was fast asleep.

CHAPTER 8

I woke up groggy and confused. The light was dim. I looked around and startled because Magnus was right there, kneeling beside the bed, looking right at me. "How long have you been here?"

"Just for a moment. Night is coming on and I was hopin' ye would come eat soon, because Chef Zach and I have a surprise for ye."

I smacked my lips. "A surprise? For me? I really need to brush my teeth first."

I checked the clock: 7:10. No wonder it looked like sunset outside. He rose from his knees and sat on the bed while I went to the bathroom.

"You might want nicer clothes."

I returned with my brush in my mouth and paste lather all over my lips. "Really? What is it?"

"'Tis a surprise."

He was wearing a nice kilt and a dark shirt, open at the neck. Really hot, lord-of-the-castle-night-time casual. I disappeared into the bathroom and sniffed my pits. Gross. I sponge-bathed all my parts and then stepped out to the hallway, naked, figuring my husband would enjoy the view. When I glanced his way it was clear from the smile on his face. I scanned through my dresses and found a little black sundress. "What were you doing while I was sleeping? I feel so much better by the way."

"I plotted your surprise with Chef Zach and then I sat with Ben for a bit." I pulled the dress on and picked some panties from my drawer and pulled them on. "And then I spent some time in prayer."

"Oh."

"I asked for guidance in these matters and think I have an answer."

"You do?"

"Aye."

He looked pensive. I went and wrapped my arms around his head. "Is it about us, are we okay?"

He nodded in my arms. "I would have asked ye this same question."

"We are, it's just been a complicated day. I know you were scared. You were just trying to get me to try harder, but Magnus you're twice my size. You're bigger, scarier, stronger, and I get that you could hurt me if you wanted to. That is the plight of being a woman, danger is inherent in loving someone. I chose you because you won't. Ever."

"I winna. Ever."

"See, we're okay. It was just the stress of the moment and you forgot what you were about."

"And you had a gentle reminder."

I smiled. "At the end of a knife point."

"You can defend thyself, ye proved it." His hands rubbed up my ass lifting my dress. He nuzzled into my chest.

My throat caught. "And you can leave me knowing I'll be okay."

He nodded and let my dress fall back down. "We should go see your surprise."

He led me from the room and through the living room. Chef Zach was leaned over a kitchen counter working on something. The room was mostly dark. Up the stairs, through the office, out the sliding glass door, and through to the roof porch. This was usually only used by the security guards but now was strung with twinkling lights. There was a small table and two comfortable chairs. Candles flickered in the center of the table and it was set with a tablecloth and china. Faint music lilted from speakers hanging from the corners of the house.

Emma pulled a chair from the table for me and gestured for me to sit down.

"This is beautiful."

"Zach and Quentin set it up."

"Where's Ben?"

"Sleeping, I've got a baby monitor on, and shush, you're ruining the magic."

Magnus pushed my chair in for me and sat across from me a smile on his face.

"You came up with this?"

"The spirit of the idea only. I told Chef Zach I wanted something special for ye. He and Emma came up with the parts."

Emma uncorked a bottle of wine and poured two glasses. "I'll be back with your appetizers." She left through the office.

"This is amazing."

"You deserv'd somethin' verra special, and we haena dined with each other in a long time."

I drank from my wine and enjoyed the warmth flowing through me. The first few moments of conversation were stilted and awkward but then something he said made me laugh. I returned a joke and a moment later we were both laughing. The appetizer arrived: warm olives, cheeses, and cured meats, and we ate happily. Magnus pulled the plate in front of him joking that he would eat it all.

"You sir, keep eating like this, ice cream at all hours, and we'll have to put you on a diet."

He laughed, jovially, "I can just go back tae Scotland and starve for a bit, will cure any paunch I gain."

I giggled and stole an olive from the plate. "Watch this." I tossed it high and caught it in my mouth. I grinned. "I have mad skills. I also feel like I got my mojo back a little."

"Your mojo?"

"My magic, my secret powers, my vitality."

"In my opinion, ye never lost it."

"You have to say that you're my husband." I stretched back and put my feet on his knee, comfortable. "Since we're reeling from your mom's bitch-move, tell me something good about your family."

His hand stroked my ankle. "Sean has a son nae much older than Ben. I was thinking of him today. His name is Gavin, a braw lad living three hundred years afore Ben yet so much alike. Screaming their heads off for the fun of it." He chuckled.

"You're an uncle?"

"Three times. You are also an aunt."

"I hadn't thought of that." I shook my head. "I never thought of that at all — your family in Scotland is my family too. I've always wanted a sister."

"My sister, Lizbeth, has a son named Jamie. He is about four years auld, and she has a wee lass named Mary."

Emma appeared on our rooftop deck to bring us the next course, New York strip steak with roasted potatoes, Brussels sprouts, and carrots. "This looks delicious," I said as a cry emitted from the baby monitor.

Emma said, "Oops! Okay, if you need anything Zach will deliver from now on." She hustled from the room.

"I can't believe they're okay with the dangerous situation today, the break in, the threats..." I said, watching her go.

Magnus said, "They arna okay with it but I believe life has been hard on them afore this. I spoke with him long this afternoon, they would like tae make it work here. I am glad he is willing' tae stay, and tis good that your priority has been tae keep them comfortable."

"I guessed life would be pretty bleak for you without Chef Zach, and speaking of that, let me tell you what happened when I came back..." I launched into the story of my return: How the house had been closed up. Why Quentin had been in jail. How I begged Zach to come home. And about unpacking the boxes and how it felt when I was putting his things into their drawers. Then I told him about the night, months later, when Emma went into labor.

Magnus and I ate and talked about our household, our family, our duties and our goals, eating our steaks, drinking wine, using my phone to call down to Zach for ketchup before Emma returned with Baby Ben in a sling, her shirt up so he could nurse, to bring us more wine.

After I was stuffed full of food, Emma and Zach both appeared to bring a platter of strawberries, slices of bananas, a stack of graham crackers, toasted smashed marshmallows, and a bowl of melted chocolate. I moaned happily. "Zach how did you get all this done?"

Emma laughed, "He has been frantic down there for two hours, you like?"

Magnus's face was hilariously excited.

"Everything has been delicious, thank you so much. And high class S'mores, yummy."

"See, I told you," she said to Zach.

"Yeah you did, I just wanted it to be perfect." They disappeared through the office. I dipped a strawberry in chocolate and nestled it on a marshmallow's gooey middle, smashed it between two crackers and held it toward Magnus. "Lean over your plate, this will be messy."

Magnus and I ate S'mores and drank and laughed and talked, and it was probably one of our best nights ever. The perfect date. And though he hadn't planned it all — he had started it for me because I had a bad day.

And that meant so much.

By the end of it I was fresh and new and hot for him. The way his arm was bound in muscles and held the S'mores so gently in his strong hands. His jawline as he concentrated. His lips as he smiled. He had a little sun on his nose from the day and when he leaned back in his chair, his knees sprawled, my feet resting on his firm thighs, I was really very very very hot for him.

"I need tae talk tae ye of something, Kaitlyn." His voice startled me.

"That sounds serious?"

"Tis serious."

My stomach dropped to my shoes. His expression had turned down. His demeanor was nervous. His *everything* was classic man tricking me with hotness into thinking everything is okay then springing with something much like — I *don't love you anymore.*

I pulled my foot from his thigh and stood.

"Magnus. Are you going to say something awful?"

"Please sit, tis nae like that."

I sat, nervously chewing my lip. "What is it then?"

He was slow to begin as if he was choosing his words, again freaking me out. "I have decided, Kaitlyn, twould be best if ye would come with me when I go back."

It took a moment for my mind to stop thinking: He's breaking up with me. And how adolescent was that — my husband says 'we need to talk' and I freak out? I would need to unpack that with a therapist probably, because that 'panicky insecure thing' was not how I wanted to be, but here I was doing it.

Speaking of panic though, my husband wanted me to go back in time with him.

"I didn't ask to go with you, I've been careful—"

"I ken ye have been verra quiet on the matter. Your silence allowed me tae think on it. After careful consideration and prayer I think twould be for the best."

"Why? I mean, I'm not sure now is the best time. My grand-mother is in a new home—"

"Your parents live here. They can see tae her. And afore ye had a verra large distance between ye, there were thousands of miles. She has had months living with ye, now a few months away twould be a'right I think."

"But the company, the money, everybody, and—"

"You have made it so Zach and Emma would be our stewards."

"I did, they can be, I just... is this because I'm scared of Lady Mairead? Because fear is not — I mean she is scary as hell, but isn't that why we have round the clock security? To protect us from — I'm just saying I'm not ready to go. It would take me some time and—"

"Tis nae because of Lady Mairead. But having ye here with Lady Mairead threatening your life — ye will bring danger tae Chef Zach and his family. Tis too much for Quentin tae guard for."

"It could be dangerous for Baby Ben?"

"I daena ken but it might be, and tis nae this only. I was already thinking on it. Tis nae fear."

"Then what is it?"

He fiddled with his fork for a moment. "Being without ye, searching for ye through time. Twas verra hard. And Mistress Hayley said we are apart too much—"

"She meant you should stay here."

"Sean needs me."

"Ah." I nodded thinking, trying to sort out how to make it happen. The truth was it would be really impractical, hard to get all the stuff I needed to go—

My husband pushed his chair back and dropped to his knees in front of me.

"Madame Kaitlyn Campbell, I have traveled for a long time to get home tae ye and I daena ken if I can leave ye again." His head was bowed, his hands at his side. "It takes all the pain I can bear tae think on leaving ye. Without ye I am but half of myself. Tis verra difficult." His eyes cast down, his lashes shadowed his face. He spoke to the ground in a stream like a prayer. "I ken it wasna be easy for ye tae come but we are bound, and I need ye."

"You need me?"

He nodded, his eyes still cast down. "Without you I am lost, always searching for ye. I canna be—"

I stroked my fingers down his cheek and he pressed his face into my hand bowing his head more, his eyes clenched tight. "I die when I am in the past. How dost ye know when tae declare me dead? You could decide it, call me dead, and I canna blame ye for it. Because I am. But I daena want tae be, I want tae live," he put his arms around my hips, his head in my lap. "With ye."

I stroked down his cheek. "I would never declare you dead, I wouldn't..."

His voice rose from the fabric across my thighs. "You will have tae someday and everyday tis true."

"You aren't dead, you're in my arms, flesh and blood."

"Aye, in your arms. If I am in the past, I am the past. If you are with me, you are my home, my future. You keep me alive."

I pulled his chin up so I could look in his eyes.

"You really feel this way?"

"I do. You ken I call ye, mo reul-iuil?"

"Yes." Our voices were whispers. His voice low and gravelly, mine alone and light on the air. "It means I'm your North Star."

"It pains me tae have ye so distant, guidin' from afar. I need ye close whisperin' your voice in my ear. You think I am leavin' easily but I canna, nae without ye. And I ken tis bleak and hard and frightenin', but I beg of ye tae have mercy on me."

Oh.

Oh.

I traced my fingers down his cheek again and nodded. "You need me to go with you, I will."

His strong arms tightened around my hips, holding me so close.

I pulled his face up cupped in my hands. "But we have to be together, Magnus. When you go get Sean, I have to go with you. I can help. I will. But you can't just take me to 1702 and drop me off at Balloch and disappear. We only have one time vessel. We have to stay together."

"Aye, and I will keep ye safe, mo reul-iuil, I promise."

I wrapped my arms around the back of his head. "I know you will."

CHAPTER 9

When we woke up, I was sprawled across his chest. Sleeping together was still new enough that we cuddled through it, and I had taken to sprawling on him using him as a pillow in some ways staking my claim. He slept pretty lightly and was usually awake when I began to wake as if he was waiting for me.

I was going to pack today to go back in time with Magnus. I had done this before, by accident of course, but today I would plan, make lists, prepare. Much of the fear was gone. I knew what I was getting into, chamber pots and evil lairds, but also my husband — I caressed my palm over his taut chest, rounded it down his shoulders, felt him nestle his cheek to the top of my head as I rubbed along his bicep and down to his hand, big, strong, capable. I nestled my hand inside of his, sheltered. He would keep me safe. He couldn't do it if I was here, alone, not really, and it was the not knowing that was making us crazy. We had promised to be whole together, forever, but had been apart most of the time and I barely knew him, still, but wanted to...

The eighteenth century was just a time. I would think of it like a vacation. With no antibiotics.

Remember to add antibiotics to my list.

As if he read my mind, his rumbling voice asked, "You are makin' a list, Kaitlyn?"

I smiled up at his face, "How did you guess?"

CHAPTER 10

I was sitting with Emma making our shopping list. "I think protein bars or something, right?"

I wrote: protein bars.

"What flavors?" asked Emma.

"I like ones that have chocolate. I think Magnus would like Cliff bars, also how about dried meat like jerky?"

I wrote: chocolate, Cliff bars, dried meat.

The good thing about Emma was that she had gotten so good at shopping for me she read between my lines. She filled in the blanks and brought back what I wanted, even if I didn't know what I wanted at the time.

"Um, what about your period?"

"It's due in two days."

Her eyes went wide. "What's your plan? You know how you get; it's not pretty."

"I need a lot of Midol, extra-strength. Also a very under-standing Highlander."

"Has he ever been around you?"

I said, "No. I managed somehow to be married to him for

almost a year without having to even discuss it. What are the odds? And what would they call it in Scotland in his time? Would they? Did they keep it a secret? Oh god, am I going to need to pull up a website and do a family planning seminar?"

Emma was amused. "He probably calls it the Curse."

"Well in my case it would be totally true. I suppose when I'm PMS-ing on the back of a horse in the 18th century I can complain about it to Magnus in detail."

She giggled. "Poor Magnus."

"Poor Magnus? It's my insides that will be mutinying. The least he can do is listen to me bitch about it."

She returned to our list. "A menstrual cup would probably be best. I'll get you one at the health food store. Some Rescue Remedy and essential oils."

"Lots of Burt's Bees lip balm. I need a locking metal lunchbox to put all the food and edibles in..."

"Why?"

"Rats."

She grimaced. "Okay, a lockable back pack for all this stuff."

I was listing furiously. "What about a filter with a water bottle?"

"I could go to REI in Jax, Zach could go with me?"

I said, "Let's send Hayley for that. I need you here to go over the paperwork. Also Zach needs to make us food today, last meals and all for a while."

I wrote: Flashlight. New hiking boots. Also: Make the dress ready. Long underwear.

Magnus interrupted us. "I have an idea, can we run through some drills?"

CHAPTER 11

a bit later we were on the beach with Quentin and Zach. "I want ye tae stand behind me like this." Magnus set me in a guard position, knees loose, elbows out, a knife in each hand.

His plan was this: if there was any trouble at all I would grab knives and get behind him. Back to back.

I would protect his back and he would protect me.

We practiced with Quentin and Zach coming toward us, sparring, circling.

Magnus fought with his sword, two-handed, and when he swung I stepped closer to his body. When his arms arced the opposite direction I followed him. It was a little like dancing. I found his rhythm. It became an improvised choreography.

When Zach came from my right I called, "left," and Magnus's sword swung to protect my left flank while I lunged toward Zach on my right.

Magnus said, "Good Kaitlyn, call out your directions." So I did, occasionally. "Right, left, left," but it wasn't always necessary. Magnus and I had a rhythm going, a flow. I felt his muscles tense.

I could feel his energy pulse, his breath quicken. It gave me clues to how and where he was about to move. Without needing to see .

My back brushed his and I felt a ripple effect as he swung again, hot and powerful. I lunged out protecting him from Zach's practiced advances, and after knocking Zach's sword away I felt Magnus arc to my left.

I twisted right and lunged just under Magnus's arm toward Quentin, and knocked his sword to the side, too.

Zach laughed, "Nice, Katie!"

Magnus was breathing heavily, a smile on his face. He nodded proudly.

I was breathing fast, hard, that had been — *awesome.* I was fired up — excited, flushed, sweaty, and I really, really, *really* wanted my husband.

Quentin said, "Need us anymore? I have some things to gather for your trip."

Magnus dragged his eyes from mine to say, "Nae, you can go. Thank ye, Master Quentin."

"No worries, I'm getting your luggage and a knife for Katie. I'll be back by this evening."

Zach said, "I'm off to get lunch started." He glanced at his watch. "Crap, looks like it will be a little late."

Magnus's chest rose and fell with his breaths. "Tis okay, I can wait for it."

"See you guys at the house." He walked up the boardwalk.

Magnus's eyes were on me, hard. He wanted me. I could see it in his expression, intense. I could hear it in his breaths, heaving.

I dropped my knives in the weapons bag and his eyes didn't move from me. "How bad do you want me Master Campbell?"

His breath sounded like a bull. "Verra bad, Madame Campbell."

He looked incapable of logic, so I took the sword from his

hand and dropped it in the bag too. Then I walked backwards to the steps pulling him along behind me. Flirting, "How bad?"

"Tis enough to say verra, because tis verra..."

"Verra verra verra badly?" We reached the top of the steps, and I turned and bolted, laughing. "Last one to the room wins!" I ran down the boardwalk with him thundering behind me. I made it to the sliding door first and opened it to our bedroom. He grabbed my hips and held them tight to his front.

I twisted around in his arms, "I beat you, you're so slow." I wrapped my arms around his head.

"I dinna want tae win—" His mouth was on mine.

I wrestled off his shirt. He tugged up the bottom of mine. It was all desperate and silly, and we were both sweaty and breathing heavy, and I was so freaking eager for him, and his yearning was right there plain under his kilt. I pressed against him with a laugh. "Oh you want me verra verra bad."

He lifted my feet from the floor and walked me to the bed, his lips pressed to my mouth. He dropped me to the mattress and I bounced giggling, quickly shoving my pants down. He shifted his kilt, fumbled with his belt under it, and dropped all the fabric to emerge naked, strong, awesome. He glistened from exertion but I only had a moment to see because he was on me, quick, hard, powerful, his body in mine, my lips on his shoulder, his salty taste on my tongue, the smell of him, god, in me, pushing, filling, and — *how much do you want me?* He was lost in the effort, me, my body. Eyes closed his body forceful, his voice a moan and not an answer, but I had my answer — *so verra verra much.*

When we finished he said, "Phwesha," and shook his head.

I chuckled and kissed him on the beating pulse of his throat. "That was yummy."

"Twas," he rumbled into my ear.

"Is this how every battle ends?"

He chuckled, low and deep. "Nae, have ye seen the men of my clan?"

I giggled. "I have."

He softened and relaxed on my body. "They wouldna look nearly as well in your wee tight pants."

I laughed so much I snorted. Which got him laughing, warm in my ear. The full light of day in our room, air conditioner humming, our glass door wide open.

Luckily no one ever walked to this end of the deck.

"Speaking of pants, your butt is out for the whole world to see." I smacked it playfully.

"Aye, tis worth it, you are laughing, Kaitlyn. Tis good tae hear. I missed your laugh."

"We aren't saying goodbye for once."

He kissed me long and sweet. "There has been too much of saying goodbye."

"I agree."

He rolled off me to the bed. "Let's shower and get some lunch. We have a great deal of packing afore the morrow."

CHAPTER 12

*B*y evening our living room held a very large pile. Too much to carry, too much to need, but all of it completely necessary. Zach planned a big dinner, a seafood bouillabaisse with crusty bread, and we sorted and packed while we received goodbye visits from family and friends. My parents came by on a quick visit before going out with colleagues for drinks. They warmly greeted Magnus and seemed surprised that he wanted me to travel with him. It went against how they imagine our relationship was — green-card based.

They accepted instructions from me: keep the business going exactly as I wanted. They understood when I explained that Magnus's castle had no WiFi and phone service would be spotty. I told them it might be months and that if they needed me in an emergency Emma and Zach were my administrators.

My father spoke with Zach. My mother managed to take my instructions without deigning to speak to him at all. Both my parents immediately went back to asking Magnus for his opinion on everything. And relentlessly continued though he asked me for every answer.

It was one big confusing, exhausting conversation, full of lies and misdirects. Part of the drama of doing business with the family I supposed. When they left after tearful hugs goodbye, I about collapsed from the drain of it all and gratefully took the beer Zach opened for me.

Hayley came by just after dinner. She bustled in and straight for Magnus. "This was not what I meant at all. I meant you should stay around, not take her with you."

I said, "That's a fair point I made last night."

"Exactly, It's not fair to leave her. It's not fair to take her!"

Magnus said, "I daena want tae live without her."

Hayley deflated.

Then she looked outraged. "How am I supposed to argue with that?"

"Exactly," I agreed. "I couldn't argue. He can't stay, so I'm going to go with him. I'll be back. It's like a trip abroad."

Hayley flounced onto the couch. "What did he say to talk you into it?"

I looked at Magnus not sure how much I could expose of his begging last night.

He gave me a half-smile and said to Hayley, "I dropped tae my knees and asked her tae have mercy on me."

"Jesus Christ you are a romantic soul. Are all the boys like that in Scotland? Fine Katie, you can go. You have to bring me a present back though, like a gold coin or something. And don't miss my wedding!"

"You haven't set a date yet."

"If you aren't back by Christmas, I'm setting it. You'll miss my wedding if you aren't back. You'll miss my nephew taking his first steps." She gestured over at Ben in Emma's arms.

"Speaking of your groom, where is he?"

She dropped her head to the back of the couch and dramatically sighed. "I can't even, don't get me started."

"What?"

"He's taken up cycling. He'll be here in a bit. It's freaking miles and I'm in the car. I'm driving here. He's coming on his bike. His bike. Like he's four years old. Plus, who's going to be my designated driver?"

Zach passed her a beer at that moment. "Baby brother is cycling? Like big helmet and tight black shorts with the padding on the ass?"

She nodded ruefully. Zach stifled a laugh.

Magnus asked, "Tight shorts?'

Hayley said, "He has these little tiny shorts. So tight. Like yoga pants. You know, Katie wears them sometimes."

"Men wear these?" Magnus smiled at me chuckling about our conversation earlier. "Where would they put their..."

Chef Zach finished, "Tatties and neeps? Oh they just tuck them in." We all devolved into laughter.

Hayley finished, "He'll be here any minute, please no laughing. It's cute how he thinks he's sexy when he's in his gear so don't spoil it." She glanced around at the pile. "Katie, how are you going to fit all of this in your tiny time machine?"

"I have no idea. I need to find a shrinker first."

CHAPTER 13

*W*e went to bed late. Friends went home with many hugs and kisses. Midnight snacks were eaten. A lot of beer was consumed. My backpack was mostly packed except for some things still strewn around that would get packed tomorrow.

Quentin gave me a small knife. It was as small as my hand and fit between my fingers. Its sheath was made to ride between my breasts inside my bodice which made me feel a little deadly and kind of sexy.

My dress was hanging in the closet hallway, waiting for me to don it in the morning. Zach and Emma and Quentin were ready to run my household, my business, my life. It was a weird feeling to know I was going away for about a week but my family and friends would experience it as much, much longer.

But I was only going away for like a week.

Easy.

Except it hurt like hell and I was not really, at all, looking forward to it. Actually I was really really scared to do it again. Pain was not my forte.

Speaking of pain, my period was coming in like a day.

I crawled into the bed dressed in a tiny T-shirt and my favorite comfortable panties and Magnus finished brushing his teeth and crawled in after me. He wrapped around my middle nestling his face into my breasts. I folded around his head, my thigh over his hips. Pulling our fluffy comforter up to our shoulders. "We will miss our bed, mo reul-iuil."

"We will." I pressed my cheek to the top of his head. "But we won't miss each other."

CHAPTER 14

*N*ext morning we had a big breakfast with Zach and Emma and Baby Ben. My nervousness was growing. There was so much to think about, to do, but then again, everything was done. I was fussing with stuff. Did I put the checkbook out for Zach? Did I remember to put my birth control pills in my pack? What about one more pair of socks?

Emma gave me a bottle of vitamins to take, "Full of B, for your, you know, epic menstrual-cycle dramas."

"Thanks." I took a couple for the day and poured a few more out to pack for later. Then I noticed another bottle of multivitamins. I poured a couple in my hand and dropped them beside Magnus's plate, piled high with oatmeal pancakes, bacon, scrambled eggs, and fruit. "What's this then?"

"Vitamins for you to take."

"What for?"

"They make you strong and healthy and fill in the gaps of your nutrition." His brow furrowed as he took a big bite of pancakes. "I daena have any gaps."

"It's not meant as an insult. It's nutrition." I went to the kitchen to look through the drawers. Would I need a fork? It would be nice to have a fork just in case.

"I daena need it, twill make me soft."

I shoved the drawer closed and looked at Magnus incredulously. "Make you soft? What the... Zach do you hear this? Magnus, polishing off a plate of pancakes thinks the multivitamin will make him soft."

Zach said, "I don't know, I have to agree. Nutrition is better from food than pills."

Magnus gestured at Zach with his fork. "See?"

"He's going to be living in 1702. I don't think some vitamins are going to hurt him!"

Magnus shrugged, "If I get used tae eatin' the magic pills what about when I daena have the magic pills?"

"Oh for Pete's sake." I slammed the drawer shut and looked around the room. There wasn't anything left to take and the bag was stuffed already. "They aren't magic,"

Magnus said, "If it upsets ye, I'll take the magic pills."

"No, it doesn't upset me, I just want..." Tears welled up and I gulped them down. "I just want one freaking thing that I'm in control of. For the next week my life is going to be dangerous and confusing, and I'd like one thing that people do just because I say so. One less fucking thing that I don't have to worry about."

Magnus pulled the two pills into his palm put them on his tongue and swallowed them down. Zach held out his hand and Emma poured in two pills and he swallowed them down.

Quentin said, "All right, me too." And took two vitamins as well.

"Thanks everyone, sorry about that. I'm going to go get dressed."

CHAPTER 15

$\mathcal{M}$agnus appeared to help with my dress. I was wearing silk long underwear. It hadn't been easy to find them in June in Florida but they were on my body. We had stretched the shoulders and cut the neck so it could be tucked inside the neckline of my bodice.

My giant wool dress still smelled a little swampy after my swim months ago.

Emma stuck her head in the room and I asked her to crank the AC up. It was blazing hot.

I watched my husband as he prepared to don his traditional kilt. A ritual that involved laying out the fabric, pleating it down the middle, weaving through a belt, laying across it, then cinching it all around. When he stood, he was wearing his skirt. It was time-consuming but at least he could do it himself.

I, on the other hand, needed someone to cinch my waist for me. But I wasn't complaining. There was something pretty romantic about my Magnus with his powerful hands, tugging at my laces, delicately pulling on my middle, breathing softly in concentration.

It was the opposite of the sexy taking-off of clothes.

Putting-on was committed, loving.

Just as I thought it, he leaned down and kissed me right on my cleavage. Oh hell yeah, sexy again.

"You are nervous?"

"Yes. Not happy at all about the mode of travel, the destination, the reason it's necessary—"

"Are ye havin' second thoughts?"

I adjusted the front of his kilt and tucked the long sides in at his waist the way he liked it. "No. I love my traveling companion, so none of the rest of it matters."

He rested his hands on my waist. I put my hands on his. "We just have tae rescue Sean. Then we will come back. After that we'll make decisions about Lady Mairead and the other time vessels together."

"I agree. And we should do this fast because I don't want to over-think it. Plus it is hot as hell in these clothes."

Quentin was driving us to the south end of the island. It was private there; we were less likely to be noticed. Magnus and I rode in the back seat, the roof up, the AC blasting. His sword across his knees, my backpack on my lap. Now and then I unzipped it to check if something was actually there. It all was. Every single thing I thought of in the past few hours, that I had room for, was in there.

I was especially proud of my new solar powered flashlight. The solar panel could also charge my phone, which I brought so I could take photos. What the hell would happen if I had photos of the 1700s? I didn't know. Zach and I speculated last night that it might create a space-time rift through the universe, but he had been a little high at the time and ultimately that was ridiculous. I was taking photos. I probably wouldn't bring on the end of the world. Probably.

Quentin pulled the Mustang over to the shoulder, half in sand. And came around to open the door for us and help with our bags. He didn't need to; we were packed very lightly considering the distance. "Boss man, see ya soon. Next time I wanna go."

"Och aye, ye would find it a great place Master Quentin, full of bonnie lasses and ancient armaments but for now I need ye tae guard the house."

"I will sir Boss. You can count on me."

I said, "And take care of the apartments. That new couple wants to move in. Their deposit is—"

"I got it Boss lady, no worries."

Sweat dripped down my forehead already. "And go to your meetings. Work your program. If you need someone to go with you, Michael will. Zach will. Emma will. Meet your probation officer. You hear me?"

He nodded with a sheepish grin.

"Okay then."

Magnus and I walked a little away from the car over a small dune to a stretch of beach that was private and nice.

We stopped and faced each other. We both had dribbles of sweat from our temples, beads on our upper lips. "It's not the vitamins that will make you soft, it's the air conditioning."

"Och aye, tis sweltering out here." He adjusted the straps on my backpack. Then took the time travel vessel from his sporran.

I gulped. This was real. I was doing this with foresight and decision. Was I freaking crazy? He took my hand. Facing each other, we huddled close. He held the vessel between us and twisted the dial while I held his forearm. It hummed to life. The markings glowed. He dialed the ends so the markings aligned. "Hold tight," he said and then he began to say numbers. "One naught eight three, twelve—"

"No no no *nooononononono* no, oh no," I dropped his hands and stepped away, "No no no, oh god, no, phew, whoa," I shook my hands out and clutched my diaphragm, taking a deep ragged breath. "Oh shit, oh no, I can't oh no no no—"

I bent over and tried to catch my breath. He might leave. He might leave without me while I acted like a chickenshit. "Don't go Magnus, don't you dare go, just—" I stood and pulled at the front of my bodice. "I just need a mo—"

"Are you okay?" His voice was quiet and rumbling and comforting and...

"Yeah, it just — I've never been good at jumping. If I think on it too long, I can't. Why's it so freaking hot?" I swiped at the sweat on my forehead. "Okay, I can do this. Let's do this. Can we sit?"

Quentin called from the car, "Everything cool?"

"Yeah, I'm just taking a moment."

Magnus sat down on the beach, crisscrossed legs. I sat right in front of him, knee to knee. We bowed our heads over the vessel and he twisted the dial again. It hummed and glowed. I wrapped my hands around his and closed my eyes.

He said "one naught eight—"

I scrambled away. "No no no, oh no no no, okay, wait, please wait. I'm still... It hurts. I'm just — I'm having trouble with the — it hurts."

"You canna go."

"I can. I can go, I can. I can do this. I can do it."

"If you canna, I will come back."

"No, you can't leave me Magnus, you can't. Don't you dare. I'm just getting my courage up. I can do this. I can do anything I set my freaking mind to. Did I start a YouTube channel? I did. Did I clunk the candlestick up against that Lord Shifty-eye's head? I did. Did I run in the middle of the night through a 18th century forest? That was me. I did that." While I recounted my heroism I crawled onto my husband's lap. I pulled up my skirts that were covered in sand and wrapped my legs around his waist. My arms under his, my hands laced around his back, I tucked my head into his chest like a monkey. Not quite heroic looking, but it was the only way I was going to go.

"Who jumped off her grandparents's dock the last day of vacation because she was too scared to do it the first day and sat around wishing she was brave enough and then finally she was brave enough? Me, that's who. I can do this." I spoke into his shirt. "I can do it."

I felt the vessel come to life resting between his hands against my lower back.

"Before you say the numbers say something romantic." I was leaving a sweat spot on his chest.

He said low and deep and only for me, "Tha gaol agam ort, mo reul-iuil is ann leatsa abhios mo chridhe gubrath. One naught three—" and I was ripped screaming from my time to his.

CHAPTER 16

J woke as if from a nightmare, heart racing, shocked, adrenaline coursing, everything hurt, writhing pain and no solace. I was in wet mossy dirt, leaves, sticks. The muck and mire of Scotland I hoped because I would just live here now forever. Because that jumping shit sucked hard.

Beside me, "Shhhhhhhhhhhhh." There must be something or somebody. I looked at Magnus's face. His eyes were clamped shut. His body wrenched in pain. His jaw clamped shut, "Shhhh-hhhhhh." He wasn't shushing me. He was shushing his body's anguish.

I remembered the time his heart stopped and panic hit me in the stomach. I wiggled closer and kissed his nose and forced the word, "Okay?"

He nodded, "Shhhhhhhhhhhhhhh." And that's all I knew for a while.

The next time I came to, Magnus was sitting up his hand on my hip guarding me while I lay unconscious. I forced myself out of my stupor and rose. The pain was still excruciating but I was on top of it. The air was freezing. I put my head on Magnus's shoulder. He pulled a twig from my hair.

"We did it?"

"Aye, we are an easy walk from Balloch."

"So what is our plan? I haven't been able to think about anything past the trip."

"We will spend the night at the castle. At dinner I will raise an army and tomorrow you and I will go to Talsworth Castle. We will rescue Sean and my army of cousins will cover our escape."

"There's a lot of unplanned stuff in there, huh?"

"Aye, we must figure it out as we go."

"Okay, we can do that. We're smart. We're brave. We just kicked the ass of time-traveling, three hundred years, like that." I snapped my fingers, and Magnus and I both groaned.

CHAPTER 17

The dining hall was much more crowded than last time I had been there. Many more men, and many more women. It seemed like a celebration of some kind or a gathering. People sat in every chair down the table and stood in groups around the rest of the room. Smaller tables were set up in two corners and they were crowded around too.

Music lilted faintly from the minstrel playing in the corner. I could barely hear it over my own breathing and heartbeat pounding loud in my ears. We approached the head of the table and I was reintroduced to the Earl and then introduced to Magnus's uncle, Baldie. He was big, gregarious, had a warm smile and welcomed us profusely.

He asked, "And where is Ewan and Sean?"

Magnus bid me go sit at the other end of the table, the one empty chair, so he could speak with the Earl and his uncle in private.

So I found myself alone in a Great Hall in 1702. My sight was faint. The room dark and crowded. The noise a mumble but also loud like a roar.

The woman to my left vacated her chair. The woman to my right turned away from me. Bored, I lifted the tablecloth. The table was a thick wood, heavy. My chair, thick wood heavy. I had an empty chair beside me and no one seemed inclined to speak to me — which was fine. I could watch. I argued in my head about whether I could pull out my phone and take a photo of the room without anyone noticing. Suddenly a plate was placed in front of me. I smiled at the young woman before she bustled away forgetting to give me a drink.

My plate contained a mystery meat and something resembling pudding. Grey.

The only thing that would make this palatable would be beer or wine.

I looked down the table at Magnus, fifteen feet away, separated by conversations, people, empty spaces, noise, a cacophony of sights and sounds. He had a plate in front of him, three men around him deep in conversation. He glanced down the table at me and gestured toward someone behind me. Within a moment a small glass of beer appeared beside my plate.

I watched him at the far end of the room. Earnest and powerful. He was one of the largest men there and also the most handsome. Commanding. He was giving the other men the bad news: Ewan had been killed. Sean was in prison.

I watched as the news filtered through the crowd, person to person. Men stood and approached the end of the table to listen and question. Occasionally people looked down at me as they discussed the news causing me to blush uncomfortably.

Yes, I was responsible.

Yes, I got Ewan killed.

Sean was imprisoned because of me.

I hadn't even thought about how that whole sordid story would seem to his family. My ears rang from the loudness of my internal noises drowning out all other noise. Soon the conversation seemed to turned to strategizing. Voices were raised. Fists were slammed on the table.

My food was rubbery though necessary. I had a stack of protein bars but I was saving them for when we wouldn't have castle food to eat. I was thirsty for water but I left my backpack in our room. Breaking out the bottle would attract attention, anyway.

Magnus rose with three other men. They crossed the room to sit and converse at a table in the far corner. He had warned me that this would take a long time. That it would be boring and I would need to stay out of the conversation. My presence would complicate it too much. When we left Balloch for Talsworth everyone knew Magnus wanted Ewan dead and now he was. We had no proof that Magnus hadn't done the deed.

There would be some who wouldn't trust him. He wanted the men to fight alongside him because they chose to, instead of being ordered to fight by the Earl. If they were fighting under orders, he would always need to watch his back.

I watched him as he spoke, his jaw set, his demeanor focused. His broad shoulders stretched his shirt. His bicep rounded as he lifted his beer to his lips. His back was to me so it was hard to guess what he was saying. He gulped and swiped at his mouth with his arm mimicking the manners of the surrounding men. I watched other groups too. The young women eating together at the end of the table. Their dresses were much nicer than my own. One woman had a baby with her and it made me wonder what Emma was doing and how Ben was; how much time had passed? Here it had only been a couple of days since Ewan had died.

In Florida, months had passed. This was something we needed to figure out, losing all of this time sucked.

Magnus's important conversation seemed to end because the intense expressions were replaced with laughs, more beer was delivered to their table. A woman approached and stood beside them joining their discussion and their laughter. Could I go over too? Should I? Magnus didn't look over, so I sat and waited for him to retrieve me.

I was wearing a pretend sporran, leather, sort of like a fanny pack. We belted it around my hips using hidden zip-ties to make it hang the right way. I unsnapped its top and looked inside, flashlight, Burt's Bees lip balm, phone —

Three young women approached Magnus and one of them put her hand on his shoulder and laughed loudly. She said something close to his ear and then nudged his arm with her hip. My heart raced. Okay, I would go over there. But that felt desperate. I would just not notice, sit here, and pretend like my husband wasn't flirting across the room with a woman much closer to his age. Since I was like 330 years old.

Tears welled up. I was all alone and—

A female voice close to my ear said, "That one is Middy. Ye needs be watchin' her with young Magnus."

"Huh, what?" I turned to a woman not much older than myself standing behind my chair.

"I could see ye noticin', just keep him close is all I'm a sayin'. Middy has been wantin' him since she was a wee bairn. She inna keen on lettin' his marriage stand in her way. I figure she thinks that a wife from far away, as ye are, is nae troublin' to her aims at all. So keep an eye on her." She beamed down at me with her brows raised. "I'm your sister, by the way, Lizbeth. I heard ye had trouble with Ewan?"

"I did, he is um, passed away, while at Talsworth."

"Och aye, me mum in her murderous castle has done tae death my cousin. Sounds about the way it goes, but I meant before ye left. Ewan had his way on ye and my brother had tae beat him near tae death?"

"True that all happened." I shuddered a bit. "And it wasn't really your mom, but her husband that killed him."

She shook her hand, dismissing the exception. "We needs nae speak of that, my mum has made her choices. Tis a hard welcome to your new home I should think. We arena all villainous. That chap over there is downright saintly." She pointed toward one young man who seemed about the age of fourteen and was quietly eating by himself.

I laughed.

She laughed and dropped into the empty chair beside me. "Thy name is Kaitlyn?"

"Yes."

"My brother Sean is still a guest at Talsworth I hear. I wanted tae ask ye, Kaitlyn, if ye think he be alive still?"

"I do, Magnus and I are going to go get him out tomorrow."

"Aye. You have a plan then?"

"We have a key to the door that's pretty much it."

"Men always want tae storm the walls, but if I were ye I would go in through the kitchen garden like a fly, buzz around 'em until they canna understand your purpose, and then dash tae the prison. Always go in at the kitchen."

"That's exactly how I escaped. I ran through the kitchen, buzzing like a bee."

She laughed, "We think like sisters already." She gestured for another beer for us both, then looked over at Magnus. "Middy has her hand on his shoulder."

"Should I draw a knife on her?"

"Tis too crass. You are his wife. She thinks ye may be a wife of convenience, nae worthy of her consideration so she is flirting with him. He daena notice much because his focus is elsewhere, on the men, on his purpose." Our glasses were delivered.

I watched a strange woman's hand rub on my husband's shoulder right where it stretched against the linen of his sleeve and kind of thought I might throw up. Middy laughed and leaned in closer toward him.

I said, "So again, I draw a knife on her?" I was only half joking.

"Nae. Now see my husband over there?" She pointed over at a big, ruddy, curly-haired, smiling lug of a man. The kind of man who looked like he would need things explained to him more than once. And wouldn't care. "You might think tis hard tae be keepin' a man like that tae myself." She giggled because right then he dug a finger in his ear and quizzically looked at the tip. "But even though nae other woman wants him, I have learned a thing about other women who are playing fast with a husband. Because I used tae be like Middy. Ye should let her go, let her get comfortable. Allow her tae think she has command of his attention. Then ye walk over and verra low say his name."

"Just say his name?"

"Och aye, he will about break his leg jumpin' from his seat, and he will break her heart for ye."

"What if he doesn't? She is awfully cute." Middy across the room giggled and flipped her hair over her shoulder. A flirtatious move that must have been used in every century.

Lizbeth looked at me incredulously. "Have ye seen thyself? Middy inna half the woman ye are. I can see it. Magnus must see it else he wouldna have married ye."

For a half-second Middy rested her head on Magnus's shoulder. Lizbeth said, "Ye must go now."

I stood. Nervous. About to walk down the whole room.

Lizbeth handed me my wineglass to carry and rose to follow me with a bit of a smile on her lips. I wove through the men and women standing around the edges of the room and alongside the table. The conversations stopped. People turned to watch where I was going. I supposed it was a little like Real Housewives of Jersey Shore or something. What I was about to do was probably the most entertaining thing that would happen here this evening.

Watching Magnus's back as I approached was nerve-wracking. He wasn't noticing me at all. He hadn't checked on me. And didn't turn as I traversed the room. I wanted him to be the kind of guy who could feel me coming. Who actually gave a shit. Crap, maybe he was a fast and loose player in 1702 — what if he was a playboy? What if — I mean, he was really hot. He must have had a lot of women. Suddenly I was questioning everything.

I glanced over my shoulder. Lizbeth was grinning. Was she a friend or a foe? Was she setting me up to fail? What if Magnus ignored me or worse — I was four feet away, two, one, very close I said, "Magnus."

And he about broke a leg jumping up from his seat.

His focus completely on me.

He took my hands in his and said, "Mo reul-iuil, I could feel ye crossin' the room, but John was tellin' a tale and—"

I looked up into his eyes. "It's okay, it's just—" My eyes glanced down at Middy behind him sitting furiously.

"Tis why I sent Lizbeth tae get ye." He kissed me and turned to his group, "I would like tae present my wife, Kaitlyn Campbell." He tucked my arm under his and we sat together as the group raised a glass in our honor. A second later Middy left her seat with a sour look and a huff.

Lizbeth smiling sat beside me. "Told you twould work."

Magnus asked me, "What dost ye think of your sister?"

"She's great, excellent advice."

Magnus asked his sister, "Where are my niece and nephew?"

"The bairns be in the upper rooms. I dinna ken twould be good tae hear of Ewan's passing and Uncle Sean be missing. Ye will bring him home brother?"

"I will, I winna rest til he is home."

"Good, Kaitlyn tells me she will attend ye to the castle. I think tis a mistake. Ye can leave her here and I will watch on her—"

Magnus pulled me closer. "We have promised nae tae leave each other. I will watch on her. Tis decided."

Lizbeth nodded as if knowingly, "Aye, and are ye with bairn yet, Kaitlyn?"

"Oh um, no, not yet."

"And how long have ye been sharing a bed? Young Magnus dost ye need some advice on the matter?" She giggled merrily.

Magnus looked unable to answer, so I said for him, "He doesn't need any advice, he's got it all perfect."

Lizbeth laughed, "Ah, a well-bed wife, nicely done brother. I dinna think ye would be capable of it!"

Magnus asked "What — why not?"

"You are too braw with your big manly shoulders. I would imagine ye would be all about the business of it and nae the consideration tis necessary for your lady."

"Och," Magnus laughed, "I am too braw tae be a good husband, then? What do ye think, Kaitlyn?"

"I think Magnus knows how to be considerate. And he knows exactly where to put his business."

Lizbeth about fell off the bench laughing. Magnus literally guffawed. We all ordered another round of drinks and continued talking together for quite a while. I really liked her. She was friendly and sisterly though she had a touch of the no-nonsense, controlling superiority of Lady Mairead. Probably more than she wanted to believe.

Lizbeth wiped her eyes on her wool shawl. "Feels good tae laugh a wee bit. I have been worried sick over Sean."

Magnus held and patted her hand. "Me too, Lizbeth, I will bring him home."

"What of the men? Is uncle Baldie attending ye? Is the Earl sending an army? Will there be a battle at the walls?"

"Nae, Uncle Baldie canna ride with us this time, but he helped me tae gather the men. And when I have Sean, I will draw out their guards and our cousins will attack. I would like tae see Lord Delapointe killed for what he has done to Ewan."

"And you. I heard ye have been whipped? Can I see?"

Magnus pulled down the neck of his shirt exposing one shoulder and a jagged scar.

Lizbeth scowled and shook her head. "Well, you are uglier now. Tis why ye have turned out a good husband, I think." She put his shirt back and patted it gently. "If you were uglier in the face ye might be as great a husband as my dear Rory." She gestured toward her husband at the far end of the table with a group of very drunk men. He was red in the face and yelling with spittle flying from his lips.

Lizbeth laughed and sighed. Then turned back to Magnus. "You will be careful. You will be starting a war and our men be fightin' already. Did ye know there is a call for them tae head out tae fight with the clans? I tell ye brother, Drummond will be the trouble of it all. You mark my words, the next years shall be verra hard. Tis why Rory and I are here. I am worried we will lose more than we care to in the next weeks. It daena sit well tis our mother on the other side of this one."

"Aye," said Magnus and squeezed her hand.

CHAPTER 18

ecause of the lateness of the hour there was only one torch outside of the Great Hall. The passageway was dark, shadowy, and ice cold. Magnus led me by the hand through rooms, down dark halls, and into a stairwell that was pitch black as if it had never seen light before.

"Careful—"

"Crap!" I stumbled on a stone step that wasn't the right height compared to the others.

"The steps arna the right size." Magnus giggled.

"You're giggling, are you drunk?" I giggled too.

"Verra."

I stumbled on another step. "I probably can't even find my flashlight. I can't see anything, why the hell is it so — someone should turn on a light."

"We like it dark so we can—" He pressed against me on the stone wall, his lips on mine, his hands pulling up my skirt.

My arms went around his head, wrapping my shawl around us both, kissing back, enjoying his warmth on my face in the bitter cold.

His hands fumbled with my skirts, and fumbled more, then fumbled with his kilt. He laughed through our kiss. "Tis confusin' me." He tugged again then gave up and slouched against me, his breath in my ear. "Too many layers. I canna get through them. I miss your wee little dresses."

"I was wondering how you would manage my long underwear and you didn't even get there."

He chuckled. "We should go tae our room so I can properly concentrate."

He led me by both hands up the stairs and down another hall to our room. It was familiar from the last time I was there. A fire burned in the hearth but it barely heated two feet in front of it.

It took a while to get me undressed enough for bed. Magnus was getting better at the laces but we kept laughing at our plight — two Florida kids in this freezing cold and then laughing at the idea that Magnus was a Florida kid. And laughing about how he wished he was wearing long underwear now too. And the lack of light to see by. And generally laughing while we struggled with my thick clothes. Then once my skirts dropped to the ground, I leapt in under the covers, still wearing my long underwear because I would never take them off, ever. Magnus scrambled in behind me.

He tucked onto my arm, his head on my shoulder, pretending to be the coldest of us both. "I brought ye a present, mo reul-iuil."

"A present? For me?"

He reached over the edge of the bed for his sporran exposing me briefly to the cold and dragged the bag to his stomach. Under the covers he rifled through it. "What is it, what is it, what is it?"

He pushed up my underwear top and placed something on my stomach. I pulled up the covers, but it was too dark to see. I pushed them down in the middle, keeping the ends of the furry hide and the wool blanket up over my arms. There on my stomach stood a Hershey's Kiss.

"You brought that for me?"

"I did, I brought a handful for ye."

"We should just look at it. In the history of the world there has never been a moment where a Hershey's Kiss stood on a woman's stomach in a castle in 1702 in the middle of winter."

"Tis a marvel and tis nae winter, tis a Scotland summer." We both laughed and when the Hershey's Kiss bounced on my wiggling stomach, we laughed even more. Finally I opened it and ate half and made Magnus eat the other half though he had meant for it to be mine alone.

Sweet chocolate melted in my mouth as Magnus's hand caressed around my hip and pulled it closer to his waist. He snuggled into my breast. I pulled the blankets around our heads and wrapped around him.

"I am glad ye are here."

"I am too." I shivered and he pushed the covers even higher over my head.

He kissed me on my neck and wriggled up to kiss me on my lips long and sweet and then sexy and deep. He rolled on me, his solid mass adding to my coverings, and our breaths and rubbing hands added to our warmth. He dragged a palm up my side, under my shirt, meeting the raised, chilled bumps of my skin with his delicious friction. He was pulling my long underwear down and accidentally dislodged the covers. I gasped, "Cold Magnus."

He paused and looked down at my nipple pushing against the silk of my shirt — he smiled then gently, slowly, pulled my shirt up in the front exposing my chest to the frigid air. "Ah see, ye are very cold here." He took my nipple in his fingertips and traced a line up and down the skin of my breasts. "God Magnus, that is..." Bumps raised all along the path of his fingers. I shivered.

"Ye are dancin' — tis me or the cold?"

I forced out the word, "You," as he leaned just above my

breast and exhaled a sigh of warm breath. I arched toward his mouth. "More."

His mouth went over my nipple and he sucked and licked and — "Are ye warm yet?" as he nibbled just a bit.

I gasped, "What — I mean yes, I mean..."

He laughed with his lips over my breast, his breath tickling me, causing me to arch even more. "You arena speaking well, mo reul-iuil." His mouth closed over my breast again and his hand went deep between my legs. "I was asking if ye are warm enough?" His chest vibrated against mine with his chuckle as his tongue caused me to squirm even more.

His lips trailed up to my throat and I recovered enough to say, "I might be a little cold still, actually."

"Och aye, the lady requires more warmin'." He went back to the business of fondling and licking and suckling my breasts and playing between my legs and drove me to the edge of a moan when he finally climbed on me, pulling the blankets with him to cover our bodies. And within the tent on our bed his steaming breath and my moans heated the space near our faces and with a bead of sweat on his temple he shoved into me — *god oh god* — his body pushing against me, my name on his breath — *Kaitlyn* — oh so warm.

I pressed the side of my face to his lips to receive the heat. His hand ran over my skin, friction and chill, pulling me closer, his name whispered to his ear — *Magnus* — rising on the crest of my moan. He was everywhere — his fingers in my folds, his lips on my skin, his strong calloused hands firm around me, moving me where he wanted, where he needed me to go, to do, to feel, and even with the uncomfortable bed and the thick blankets and the icy cold it was awesome. I couldn't imagine wanting to be anywhere else in the world or time than here with him.

When we finished he gave me an arm for my head. I would definitely need to sprawl on him tonight because this bed was really no more than a wood plank, the feather mattress little more than an insult. Like I was dumb enough to be tricked. I was not.

I ran my hand up and down his chest and down and around his bicep, thinking about how magnificent he was, how handsome, how powerful. In my time and his and then without planning to I asked, "What's up with that girl Middy?"

He rose his head up to look down at my face. "That little flitting midge around my shoulder?"

"You know who I mean. The girl flirting with you. You're not dumb."

He chuckled. "I am nae dumb. Middy has been after me for many years."

"So what, you don't like her or something? She's really cute."

"She is just a lass."

I humphed. "What does that make me?"

"You are my motherfucking matriarch." He chuckled.

I groaned.

"You daena like that? Tis what ye said."

"I know, but it makes me sound old. She's so young, and I'm like three hundred years older than her."

He raised his head to see my face again. "You are jealous of Middy? How can this be? You are Kaitlyn Campbell. It daena make sense!"

I pouted petulantly. "I just didn't like how she touched you. It made me nervous. Like what if you want her? What if she can tell?"

"Tell I want her?"

"Men like the pursuit, the chase, and you never had to chase me. Before you even liked me your mom forced you to marry me. Maybe you'll get bored and like someone else, someone who you need to work at winning."

He chuckled low and deep in the air over my head. "You are

being unreasonable. If I want tae pursue a woman, why would I pursue Middy; she has been chasin' me for years?"

"Yeah, but you know what I mean. You married me because you were forced to, by your mom. And she is not a nice person. Maybe you'd rather be with someone that doesn't remind you of your mother's contract—"

"First, tis an arguable point, I have married ye in front of God. This conversation goes against the vows I made tae ye, Kaitlyn. Why would I break my vows tae pursue a girl, who I will mention has the brains of a stone wall, and lose my family and my home, tae be a sinner? I have never heard ye say such a silly thing."

I sat quietly for a second. "I know. I just got worried. I never thought about what you gave up to marry me. That you might have a girl you like here in Scotland. You might have given up falling for someone you got to pursue, instead of someone like me that you were forced to marry."

He shook my head off his arm shocking me but then wriggled down in the covers so we were face to face. In the dark gloom of the room, barely able to see each other except for a soft faint glow from the fire behind me.

"You think I was forced tae marry ye?"

"I have the contract — wait," My eyes went wide. "I don't even have the contract anymore. Is Lady Mairead a witch? I never thought any of this before, and now I'm worried you love someone else. Is our marriage over because the contract was burned?"

"What is goin' on with ye? First, I am forced tae marry ye, then I am breaking my vows in love with someone else and now our marriage is over? Is the blood pudding disagreeing with ye?"

"Ugh, that was blood pudding?"

He shook his head slowly. "Kaitlyn, I have pursued ye. You

had men between your legs before me. Ye werena mine for the takin', I had tae win ye."

"Really, you thought so?"

"When I met ye, I couldna stop thinking about ye, wanting tae see ye, dreaming of ye."

"You did?"

"You were surrounded by men though. Master Cook had his hand on your thigh." His arm went around me and pulled me to his chest. His voice was low, his cadence slowing, and growing sleepy sounding. "I had tae figure out what that meant and how tae win ye from him. There were some desperate moments, mo reul-iuil, where I feared I would never have ye, and that I couldna have ye. That ye dinna notice my agony daena mean I felt it less."

"But what about the contract?"

"I would have preferred tae win ye myself but Lady Mairead forced ye tae sign the contract. Tis nae me that was forced, ye ken." He added, "I was furious. But I think I would have won ye in the end. I am glad of the result however it happened."

"Me too. I don't know why I got so jealous."

"Tis funny ye are more worried about losing me to a girl in the Great Hall than the guards of the castle we plan tae storm on the morrow."

"I have a lot of experience with losing out to other girls."

"Tis another life, different men, better nae think on it." He pulled the cover up to my ears and wrapped us both up under it. "You are warm enough?"

I nodded, snuggled into his arms. And soon enough we were both asleep.

CHAPTER 19

The following morning was freezing. I waited in the ice cold bed while Magnus stoked the fire and wrapped in his kilt. Then he helped me dress right beside our fire, discussing our day, the plan, our list.

"We will get there by nightfall. I have tae spend the morning helping the men get ready. They will be just behind us." He tightened the top of my bodice's laces.

"I have the flashlights. We'll go in through the kitchen." I adjusted my breasts in the bodice. "Man I'm hungry."

"There should be food this morn, the men will be needin' a bite afore they go." He pulled the laces and tied them tight.

"You really think you can find your way to the prisons? You can find him?"

"I have a vague idea where they kept me. I can find it."

I turned around and he wrapped the tartan around my shoulders. "Ready?"

"Ready."

The day was boring after that. We ate but Magnus mostly had to talk with the gathering men. The food was filling though bland and dry. I was really excited about the chocolate chip bar I would eat on horseback in a few hours. Magnus's conversations were boisterous and hard to figure out. The other men spoke loudly, sharply, and most of the time in words I didn't understand. We all went down to the stables in twos and threes and then there was work involved in packing up the horses. Magnus had me sit to the side in a pile of hay. It was warm enough and I could watch the bustling activity without getting in the way.

I snuck my phone from the top of my bag and took two photos: One, the misty Scottish fields, ten men, and a couple of horses. Two, the activity of preparing to ride into battle.

Soon enough I was behind Magnus on his horse, holding on. My head rested on his strong back and we were headed to Talsworth with a small army behind us.

CHAPTER 20

$\mathcal{T}$he field was wet, dragging down my skirts as I raced across it. Magnus raced just behind, his breath coming in puffs. It was dark. We were using the cover to get to the door of the kitchen where dim light spilled into the kitchen garden. On our foreheads we wore headlamps but we had yet to turn them on waiting for the moment when we would be in the lower stairwells of the castle.

First, we had to barge into the kitchen and storm across the room for the stairs.

It worked.

We startled the women so much they stood still while Magnus yelling and apologizing for our intrusion tried to look startling yet warm and invited. He and I both raced through the room to a door — a stairwell — *up or down?* I paused for barely a moment. Magnus urged, "Down," and I was descending as fast as I could go without falling. My heart raced in my ears.

It was very, very dark. I stumbled and put my hands out to the wall to stay on my feet.

Magnus's voice: "Pull your knife."

I pulled it from the sheath I wore at my waist and held it in front of me blindly. I couldn't see anything at all.

"Keep going."

When my feet hit the ground floor, Magnus rounded to my front. He held his arm out protectively and I pressed behind him against the wall. He shifted to the left and I knew to follow him close like we discussed. I was his shadow. If he moved left or right I moved with him, so close he could feel me.

We turned a corner and another. I paid attention to the route. We had discussed this thoroughly. When we escaped with Sean, we both had to remember how to get out. In case we were separated. I really, really, hoped we wouldn't be separated.

We reached the end of a corridor. Magnus stopped, arm out protectively safeguarding, and peered around the corner.

He quickly pulled back and nodded. I fumbled in my bag for the keys gripping them in my right hand with my knife in my left. Magnus raised two fingers and then put his hand on his head-lamp. We nodded together and blazed our lamps and ran. Magnus was in front, me behind, running down the hall toward the two shocked guards.

By the time I reached the door, Magnus was in a full blown sword fight behind me. Grunts and blows with clanging steel on steel. It echoed through the hallway while I fumbled with the key in the door's lock. Now see, this might have been something to practice — *Calm down. Stay calm. Get the key in the lock. Turn it. Right or left?* I tried both.

A guard's hand grabbed at my shoulder yanking my shawl. I turned in time to see Magnus yank the guard away and slam him against the wall.

I frantically turned the key — *comeoncomeoncomeon* — Finally, the lock clunked and I shoved my shoulder against the heavy door. It creaked and groaned open.

I raced into the room. "Sean? Sean?"

His voice emerged through the darkness. "Who is that?" My light blared on his face.

I flicked it off throwing us into pitch black nothingness. Over my shoulder Magnus's light was still shining, lighting his battle with the last guard but then with a lunge forward Magnus's dirk shoved into the man's side. Magnus pulled it free by shoving the guard's body away with his foot. He stepped into the prison cell.

I reminded him, "Turn off your light."

Sean asked, "Magnus?" He sounded confused.

"Och aye, climb tae your feet brother, we are the rescue." Sean didn't have to be asked twice. He jumped to his feet.

Magnus picked up a knife lying beside one of the guards and passed it to Sean. Then we formed a line, Magnus in the front, me in the middle, Sean last. We raced back the way we came.

My heart was pounding. We stopped for a quick moment on the steps, half up and down, to try to settle our breathing. I wasn't sure mine could calm. I held Magnus's arm and counted slowly, trying to get on top of my coursing blood. Sean was focused and active. We had thought Magnus might need to carry him but he hadn't been cruelly injured. I marveled that he cooperated so reflexively. He instinctively knew to face down the steps while we rested, and then when Magnus nodded, he dropped into line behind me while we ascended to the kitchen.

At the top door a woman accidentally collided into Magnus as we stepped into the kitchen. She screamed. Magnus began his loud apologizing but another woman screamed too and then another. They were definitely sounding the alarm. *Shitshitshit.* I fumbled with my headlamp's power button. Once I turned it on, I leapt wildly, crazily, yelling like a banshee shining the bright light around their shocked faces. Women cowered against the wall, terrified of me.

Then the three of us raced through the room to the garden.

As soon as we escaped the kitchen, the women began to loudly scream again calling for help.

Magnus yelled, "Go, go, go."

And I raced to the trees as fast as my legs would move.

CHAPTER 21

*W*e barreled through the underbrush probably where I entered these same woods months ago. Though in this timeline it had only been a few days. We didn't follow my path around the castle though, instead we scrambled over rocks and around trees aiming for a predetermined place deep in the woods.

The Campbell men were coming up from the south and would meet us but this would have been a lot easier with a phone. Or a two-way radio. Magnus reached for my backpack, pulled it from my shoulders, and slung it on his own. And we ran. Sometimes I had to stop to walk catching my breath. Magnus would slow beside me but then he would wordlessly tug my hand, and we would run again.

Then the forest was so dark it was impossible for me to see anything. Magnus slowed and whistled like a bird. He listened. Sean listened. I couldn't hear anything over my racingpoundingflooding insides. Magnus held out his arm and I wrapped around it so he could lead me because I was basically completely blind. He and Sean picked our path around trees winding our way through the deep woods. Somehow Magnus seemed able to sense where he was going. Again and again he stopped, whistled, and listened. Until finally when I was past the point of fear and worry and about to ask, "Are we lost?" An answering whistle sounded through the trees.

We turned course to the left. Eventually we came across one of our men, a horse and another man, and another. Relief washed over me. We were behind the line.

CHAPTER 22

*M*agnus, Sean, and I hiked farther away to rest. We leaned under a tree, Magnus offered me his side, and I collapsed across his lap. I laid there in exhausted shock, too adrenaline pumped to sleep. Too exhausted to sit up. Plus, the sweat and the temperature worked against me and I froze numb. Magnus wrapped my tartan around me and his legs. He wrapped his own tartan around his shoulders and me.

I lay there in a stupor listening to Magnus and Sean talk. Their voices were thick, their words different, so I couldn't understand much. It lasted for a while but soon their words sounded angry, short, clipped, and growling.

Then Sean uttered something in English. My ears pricked, alert and listening. "...because she is a witch."

Was he talking about Lady Mairead — or me?

Magnus's arm tightened on my shoulder. "She has saved your life."

Me. Oh crap.

I tried to remain totally still, pretending to sleep under Magnus's protective arm — Magnus's body tensed. It made me feel scared. Sean's reply was low and guttural, but I couldn't make it out over the panic filling my ears.

Magnus said, his voice barely audible, "I canna explain these flames, brother, but she is nae a witch. The part of the world she comes from has these lights. Tis nae magic, tis a flame from the New World. I will give ye one, ye will see—"

"I daena want one."

Magnus's voice was whispered but firm. "I promise ye, tis different from the spells of our mother. Lady Mairead is a witch, I will agree, but Kaitlyn, your sister, tis nae. You must believe it."

Sean grunted.

"I promise ye, when ye talk tae her in good fun over dinner, ye will see. She has much the bearing of Lizbeth, the same kind of humor. And I think ye will find in her the piety of Maggie, your wife. But Kaitlyn is nae from here, I need your help protectin' her."

Sean said something I couldn't understand.

"I need your word on your dirk that ye will protect her if I canna. You will remember well what happened to Auld Sib, Lizbeth's midwife. Twas nae fair to try her. You ken this, we talked of it at the time. You have tae protect Kaitlyn, same as I would protect Maggie. I would protect her with everything I have. Promise ye will speak for Kaitlyn as family. She has saved your life."

Sean sat for a long dreadful moment. Then he said, "Och Magnus, aye, ye have my word."

"Good."

They sat quietly for a moment.

Magnus asked, "You daena want one of the lights?"

Sean chuckled. "Ye should hide them, tis too hard tae explain."

Magnus chuckled, his hand relaxed on my shoulder and

stroked up and down on the linen of my shirt. Calming me, letting me know the danger had passed. Warming my skin.

He and Sean talked of Ewan and the coming battle, their mother, and whether Lord Delapointe had survived. Slowly I fell asleep.

CHAPTER 23

agnus nudged me awake in the still middle of the night. He whispered, "We need tae be up, the fight will begin at dawn." The soft rustling surrounded us of men waking, rising, horses whinnying, and the near frozen ground crunching underfoot.

"Why don't we just return to Balloch; we have Sean?"

Magnus's voice was quiet though he spoke strongly as if it was for the benefit of a listening cousin instead of me. "We canna allow the death of Ewan tae stand. And we must meet them at their own gates instead of allowing them tae follow us to our own."

"But you and I could go, right? We got Sean out. We can return to Florida?"

He spoke very quietly. "I canna leave before the fight. Sean heard some of the men questioning my role in Ewan's death. I must stand with them today."

"What — but it's dangerous, what if something happens — what about me?" I held the tartan tight around my shoulders, and I had to pee. It was hard to concentrate.

"I will keep ye nearby, hidden, and safe. I have never lost a fight yet."

It was dark, really dark and this whole idea was insane. "I have to go to the bathroom."

He led me about three feet away and turned his back while I pulled all my skirts up, shoved down my long underwear, and somehow managed to clutch them all around under my arms while I peed. I kind of needed to poop too. I also really needed a good cry. I was hungry, cold, and exhausted.

I was done with this whole errand. But also, I did this, I was doing this. We were just still in the middle of it. I had to keep my spirits up and my focus sharp. I only had to wait a few more hours for this to be done-done. Then Magnus and I would go home because this was just a thing to finish.

I dropped my skirts and stood. "Okay, what next?"

Magnus looked over the two spots on my body where I carried blades to make sure they were easily accessible. Our horse was on the other side of the woods where we left it earlier, but there were two extra horses here for Sean and Magnus to ride. He slung my backpack to my back and unzipped it to check its contents. He fished out a protein bar for me, one for him, and passed one to Sean.

"What's this?"

"Food from the New World."

Magnus showed his older brother how to open the foil wrapper and peel it away from the bar. Also how to eat it in bites.

His brother's eyes opened wide at the taste. "Tis good!"

I laughed to myself. Sugar and salt must be an intense experience when someone so rarely if ever ate it.

I asked, "Should I pass them to everyone? I mean, I only have a few but..."

"Tis verra kind of ye tae offer, but some of these men daena deserve your kindness, Kaitlyn. There are mercenaries here, ruffians, ye must be careful nae tae show them the contents of your bag. And keep it on ye verra close."

"Oh, okay."

"You can trust Sean. Daena trust anyone else, ever."

The men, taking care to be quiet, led the horses to the edge of the woods. We remained just within the tree-line facing the fields in front of Talsworth castle.

I whispered, "What are we waiting for?"

"The castle guards will head this way with the first streaks of dawn."

It was still very dark but the grey hue of morning was beginning to brighten the landscape bit by bit. The surrounding men climbed on their horses. Men loaded rudimentary guns. Magnus pulled me behind a tree. "I must be quick. The guard is comin'. You are safe here, daena move—"

I felt seriously panicked. "How will you find me?"

"Tis a Yew, the only one in this part of the forest. Twill be easy tae find. The field is right there." He pointed toward the castle. "You will be able tae see me, but ye must stay hidden."

"Oh. Yeah, okay."

"I winna be long." He swung up on his horse and rode away meeting the other men and with a "Hie!" they thundered from the trees to the field beyond.

From my place behind the trunk of a tree I saw the Talsworth guard riding from the castle meeting them at full speed. Dawn had barely arrived. The air was chilled cold and still. Hundreds of horse hooves thundered across the near frozen grass and the yells of men filled the air. They were pushing their horses and forcing themselves forward. And then a couple of football field lengths away from where I stood the two armies met in the field and I begged the universe to keep him alive.

CHAPTER 24

I watched what I could. Blades were swinging. Loud clanks and clangs had my nerves on edge and then shots were fired. I shrieked and clapped my hands to my ears, terrified. If I watched I panicked until I convinced myself it was just like a movie. Like Captain America but on horses in historical Scotland. That body on the ground would get up once the director called, "Scene!" That game of pretend only worked for like two minutes.

The battling mass of men shifted closer to where I stood hidden in the trees. What if they had to retreat? What if the battle was fought through these trees? I needed to be ready, watching, and alert.

I kept my bag on my back. I sat but changed my position to a crouch as the men came closer still. Clouds of dust surrounded them. The sounds of battle filled the morning: clanging swords, guns firing, yelling, and wailing from the ground. Horses trampled over bodies on the field.

I couldn't see Magnus.

I searched the battle, raising on tiptoes, and alternately

ducking behind the tree. It was so hard to find him across the wide distance and through the crazed activity.

I found him at the far edge. He was off his horse swinging his broadsword, in a full — oh god, he was almost hit from behind. I bent over holding the tree to steady myself with my eyes clamped shut. I talked myself out of running to protect him with my tiny blades clutched in my hands.

I swore to God right then and there that I would practice fighting when I got home, *really*. I would become a badass woman warrior. I liked running and that kickboxing class I took had been really fun.

Then again, who was I kidding? Even with the skills, there wasn't anyway to kickbox in this dress. Next time I would come to the past all badass, and I would need to wear pants.

If there would ever have to be a next time.

Magnus stumbled, then rose yelling. He charged the man he was fighting. Please please please let him be okay, please. He swung his sword and the man fell to his back. Magnus jumped over another body, leapt through the air, and entered a melee on the other side of the field. I couldn't watch anyone else. I hoped Sean was okay, but I couldn't scan the fight for him. I could only concentrate on Magnus as if my eyes kept him alive.

Plus it was difficult to tell who was on the opposing side. Who was on our side? There wasn't a uniform. A man stumbled from the group, dropped his sword, and lurched toward the forest. He was holding his shoulder. Dragging his foot. He sprawled to the ground only fifteen feet from where I hunched cowering behind the tree.

Lizbeth's husband, Rory.

I raced from the woods and slid to my knees beside him. Blood spread in a red bloom on his shoulder. I peeled back his shirt — a deep wound. His eyes were shut, his lips muttering, and his skin pale.

"Hi, I'm Kaitlyn, I'm married to Young Magnus. We haven't met yet...officially, but your name is Rory?" I used my blade to cut a piece of linen from the hem of my skirt. I folded it and pressed it on his wound. He winced and groaned in pain. I pressed and considered the first aid supplies in my bag — did I remember duct tape? I had joked about bringing it, but did I? His eyes opened and he looked around panicked. Blood was soaking through the cloth covering my hands. His eyes were wild, his lips and skin pale. He grabbed my wrist, tight. I tried using my calming voice. "That would make me your sister in a way because Magnus is..."

A dark shadow crossed over us — I turned — a soldier, his sword raised — swinging down at me. I screamed. Then Magnus was there, his sword swinging up, halting the blade, driving the soldier back, and chasing him with broad strokes and lunges until Magnus's blade went through him. The guard dropped to the ground.

I had to remind myself to breathe.

I needed to get Lizbeth's husband to the trees. I checked under the cloth. It was bleeding heavily. He was moaning and writhing. I hooked my hands under his shoulders, heaved him up, and dragged him across the ground. Drag, rest, heave again, drag, rest, with a lot of dramatic complaining for my part. "Wow, are you like a fucking giant?" Drag, rest, heave. "Maybe you're only eating carbs? Is that what it is?" Heave, drag. "Goddamnit, seems like the forest was closer a second ago. Why the hell is it so far away now?"

One last drag and I collapsed on my butt. My eyes were drawn across the horribly violent battlefield to the castle. Up on the high wall a woman stood watching the battle below.

My hair raised as a chill crossed over my skin. She looked like Lady Mairead but it was a long distance. I couldn't be sure. I pressed my hands back to the cloth on his wound. "You're going to be okay because you're Lizbeth's husband. You have kids right?

You're a dad. You have to stay with me. I have some medicine I can probably..." I dropped my backpack to the ground and fumbled with the zipper.

All the while thinking, "It couldn't have been Lady Mairead. I mean, it was her home, but Sean was held prisoner there — would she imprison her sons?" I needed both of my hands for this zipper. I ripped it open and rustled around inside of it.

I thought we were fighting Lord Delapointe, but was this battle really against Lady Mairead? Lizbeth's husband clutched my hand. "Take care."

With a gurgling noise his body stilled —

An arm grabbed me around the waist and lifted me from the ground.

CHAPTER 25

*K*icking and screaming I was bodily thrown across the front of a horse, against the crotch of some strange man. With my head hanging down, my left arm was wrenched behind my back. My right wrist was gripped hard, a rope wrapped around it tight, and it was bound to my left wrist. I screamed and struggled. "It hurts! Stop! Please!"

A man's voice above me yelled, "Hiye!" and the horse galloped, pummeling my stomach as I banged up and down against the animal's shoulders. My cheek repeatedly banged against the man's thigh.

"Please, who are you, where are you taking me?" Tears streamed from my eyes, up my forehead, following gravity, headed for the ground. "Please, it hurts," I begged. I started to slide forward and a knee butted my forehead pushing me back.

Beside my horse was another, its legs a blur of motion — the only thing I could see besides the ground. Behind us, by the sound of the hooves, were at least three more. "Please." My voice became a whisper, because there was no one who seemed to be listening, no one to beg. My voice was lost in the side of the beast.

We left the woods and raced across a field and then on and on and on until I lost my consciousness as a last resort.

CHAPTER 26

I woke up hours later laying in a heap, freezing, my hands still bound, my mouth in dirt, dirt in my mouth. Freaking dirt from 1702 in my mouth. I spit and raised my head to look around. A circle of five men crouched near a fire. One glanced my way and another man said something I didn't understand. They all laughed.

"Where's Magnus? Magnus Campbell? Who are you, and why am I here?" I wanted my voice to sound outraged but instead it sounded shaky and scared. "Where's my husband? I'm married to Magnus Campbell — where is he? Are you taking me back to Balloch?"

They laughed more and continued on with their discussion.

More pressing I had to pee. It was all I could think about. "I have to go to the bathroom; I need my hands." One guy glanced at me. He was a hulking dude, red-haired, fat-cheeked. His nose was red, pitted, and bulbous in all the wrong places.

He grumbled, tossed his plate of food on the ground, and lumbered toward me. He fiddled with my ropes, letting them fall to the ground. And shoved me, just to be a dick. My stomach muscles were so sore and my wrists were raw. "Where are we? I demand to know." I stretched out my arms, man, that hurt.

One of the guys said something that sounded like, "Cally," which wasn't helpful at all. I tugged at my bodice for air and gave up making sense of my predicament because I really did have to urinate and I was going to go right there and then my legs would be wet and that would suck.

I strode to the edge of the clearing, crouched behind a tree and peed. After I peed I sat down and cried. I didn't know where the hell I was — what I was doing here? How long had we been riding, was I kidnapped? Was that even a thing in 1702?

I checked the sheath at my waist. My knife was gone.

My backpack. Shit. It wasn't on my back. I didn't see it near, or on, or around the horses...

I took it off.

When I was pressing the cloth to Lizbeth's husband's shoulder, I took it off. Because it had been constricting my movement. Because I was going to look through it for duct tape.

I was the biggest dumbass in the world.

And it slammed into me — I was dead.

Completely.

Irretrievably.

How far had we traveled while I was passed out on the horse? In what direction? How would Magnus ever find me? In the pouch around my waist I had my phone. A pad of paper and a pen.

The red-haired man shuffled over and growled, "Get up, we have tae move."

I pulled the knife from my bodice and pointed it at him from my place in the dirt. "Don't come near me. You tell me where Magnus is, right now."

He laughed, great big guffaws of laughter.

"What's so funny you fucking monster?"

He shook his head. "You have just shown where ye keep your blade."

"Oh yeah? Well... I might not be — you're still an ugly monster. I'm calling you, McBulbous, because you have a stupid fucking nose."

"Get up."

When I refused to stand, he lifted me around my waist, tossed me over his shoulder, and carried me to the horse. I struggled, but my heart wasn't really in it. This guy, McBulbous, he was in charge of me now. Because where would I run? Nowhere. This was it.

He threw me like a sack over the back of the horse again. "Please let me sit up, it hurts."

He climbed behind me on the horse and said something I couldn't understand to one of the other men.

"Are you trying to kill me?"

His arm grabbed me roughly and cartwheeled me up to a sitting position and then with jerks and yanks and painful grabs, he tied my hands together with a length of rope.

He was so gross. He smelled like a dog and his breath smelled like a constant belch and his arms were around me while we rode. I huddled, holding my elbows in, my head down, trying to be as small as possible so he wouldn't touch any part of me. But I wasn't fooling myself; McBulbous was literally right there, everywhere.

Hours passed and night was coming on.

The men led us into a valley. From the trail above I made out at least a dozen little thatched-roof shacks dotted around fields. Low stone walls weaved between the green patches of land. "Where are we?"

McBulbous grunted stinking shit-breath on my neck.

We approached one of the larger houses and the men tied the

horses to a fence near a stone wall. When I was ordered to drop to the ground. I refused. Instead I stared straight ahead.

McBulbous ordered me again, then yanked my arm pulling me from the horse. I screamed. Without my hands to break my fall my shoulder hit the ground, hard. Laying in the dirt I yelled, "You suck, you're the biggest stupidest monster in the history of the world." He grabbed me up by my elbow and shoved me inside the low door of the house.

The big large room was dark except for a low fire at one end. An old man, bent and gnarled, sat on a stool close beside the coals stirring something in a pot. He grunted when we walked in and seemed not to care about my presence at all.

My captors filled the room and sprawled all around on the floor. There was a pig in the room. Some chickens were scratching around too close to my feet.

It smelled like a barnyard. Like a barnyard where the farmer has stopped giving a shit kind of barnyard.

Our host spooned something gray from the pot into a clay bowl and thrust it towards one of the men.

The clay bowl was passed from man to man. It was refilled and passed again. They all ate from it, whatever that gray stuff was, and then finally it was passed to me. About a half cup of congealed gray something was at the bottom of the bowl. Some kind of grain mushed with milk, I hoped. It was cold and tasted disgusting but I was so freaking hungry and thirsty, so freaking thirsty. I shoveled the food into my mouth and licked the inside of the bowl.

The men seemed to think this was funny. One of them handed me a beer. I gulped it down, and groaned as the liquid filled my body. I wanted, needed another — to numb myself. I figured alcoholism might be the only way to survive this, but what was there to survive for? Life in the 1700s sucked, hard. Without Magnus I was better off dead.

The old man of the house passed through the room. "Help me." I held out my bound wrists.

He kept his eyes averted and walked on by.

Then my captors ignored me.

It was probably safer that way. As ugly as McBulbous was, the other men were horrid looking. Dirty. Actually bloody. They stank. And dumbass McBulbous seemed like he was the smartest of the lot. He was the only one who seemed to know English.

I didn't want to say anything. I kind of hoped they might forget about me, but the endless loop in my head — where was Magnus, where was Magnus, where am I, what was going on — was making me feel crazy.

Plus, I was so thirsty. "I need another beer."

McBulbous, lying against the opposite wall, grunted. He passed a mug to me through three other men. One who took a long drink from it. I still drank it because what else could I be worried about anymore?

I raised my voice trying to sound courageous. "What happened to Young Magnus Campbell?"

McBulbous grunted, "Dead."

I put my head down on my knees and cried for a long, long time.

The men spoke amongst themselves, laughing, disinterested.

I sniffled and interrupted them. "Where are you taking me?"

"Away."

"I am Kaitlyn Campbell. I am the niece of the Earl of Breadalbane. My brother is Sean Campbell. My sister is Lizbeth Camp—"

"I know all this." McBulbous waved me away as if I was insignificant. "Lady Mairead has told us."

Oh.

"So be quiet, else we will make ye quiet."

CHAPTER 27

I slept in a ball on the cold hard floor of a filthy cottage. By cold I meant fucking freezing. By filthy I meant the pig was wondering when the maid would show up. By hard I meant this was beyond what I was capable of surviving. The air was warmed by the breath and sweat and farts of so many disgusting pigs and real pigs that I wondered if I might pass out from the gas. Plus I needed to pee. My body was pissing me off. I was thirsty and needed to urinate at the same time. I needed to pee for about five hours by the time it was dawn enough for everyone to stand and eat some brittle bread. I was offered a small hunk. I chewed it down without anything to drink.

McBulbous untied my hands so I could use the bathroom, and I went and urinated in a field behind a rock wall. I scanned the horizon. Far away people dotted the fields. I considered yelling, "help!" but the wind was blowing towards me. There was no way they would hear me. And what farmer would interrupt his work and come running to fight five men because some Foreign woman yelled for help?

I could run, but McBulbous was about eight feet away.

I was forced onto the horse. We rode for a long way. An hour out I asked, "If Lady Mairead told you to take me — I still don't understand where."

"She said tae take ye tae Glasgow."

"Is she paying you? Because if she is, my uncle, the Earl of Breadalbane, will pay more. I'm sure of it. If you'll just take me to see him..."

"I will get paid after I leave ye in Glasgow. Or I can leave ye here by the side of the road and nae think on it a bit, but I am going this way, anyway. If ye keep running your mouth though, I will leave ye in a second."

Oh.

I sat on the back of the horse as it walked its steady pace trying to decide if I was better off in an 18th century port city or an 18th century village? And how 'better off' was not a phrase I could apply to my life anymore.

I dozed, huddled over my aching sides, numb in every way. Until about twenty minutes later when I felt the first blasted, painful cramp of my period. It was beginning. My uterus saying, "Why hello Kaitlyn, remember me? I've decided to wring you out from the inside while you're being people-trafficked in the eighteenth century. It will give you something else to focus on besides your eminent doom. And hey, maybe it'll be so awful, like that time five months ago, that you'll be begging for the end. Okay? Here goes—"

And oh god, it really, really sucked.

About forty minutes later I was crying. My guts were sloshing around while also crimping and burning, and I was running hot and cold, feverish. I whimpered trying to stay on top of the waves of pain.

I needed to go to the bathroom. I begged them to stop. Finally McBulbous all but threw me off the horse. I went crashing to the ground, tweaking my ankle pretty good. Shaking, I stumbled to the side of the road and the world went all dark in a tunnel around my vision like I might pass out while defecating. It hurt my stomach to hitch up my skirt and my legs were so weak I could barely hold myself in a crouch.

I found a giant leaf and used it to wipe myself. But I had nothing to stop the flow of my period down my white long underwear legs. My menstrual cup was in the backpack lying beside Lizbeth's dying husband. Was it twenty feet away from my dying husband too? God. I had to get back there. I had to get to the bag. If Magnus's body was there, maybe I could go back in time and save him before he died.

I was forced onto the horse again. I rode waves of pain. A bit later I began dry-heaving. It didn't help. It kept getting worse and worse.

I collapsed on the neck of the horse in a state of semi-consciousness. My uterus felt like it wrenched around itself. I gagged and heaved some more and I guess McBulbous decided to take some pity on me. He spoke loudly to the other men and they all rode their horses off the trail into a field. He dropped off the horse and yanked me down, shrieking, to the cold ground. I decided I should probably just pass out. Wake up in two days when this was over.

I half-expected them to ride away, but they apparently decided it was a good time to take a break. There was a bit of sun. They sat ten feet away in the field, pulled food from their sacks, and ate without offering any to me. Not that I could have eaten.

They did talk about me as I swam in and out of consciousness. I saw them look over at me lying in the fetal position in the dirt. They went back to talking and ignoring me.

About an hour later they stood, stretched, and began gathering their things to ride some more. I sat up, trying to get control of myself. "How much farther is it?"

McBulbous grunted.

"I'm really thirsty."

"Get on the horse. Or stay here. Is nae matter tae me. Ye would be unable tae survive the night, anyway. Twill be cold as a gravestone."

I got on the horse.

We rode for hours, me crying, passing out, writhing, fitful, and broken-hearted. We were headed away, and I was lost. I couldn't even think straight. I should've run away yesterday. As soon as I had the chance. I should have run, and now I was so far away that I would never get back. I didn't even know how to ride a horse or survive a night or speak the language.

I realized the men were talking about me. I tried to pay attention — they seemed to be discussing what to do because I was such a pain in the ass. Apparently my captors were beginning to believe they would be better off if I was dead.

That's how freaking dire my situation was.

And I couldn't do anything but clutch at my stomach and groan as the horse bounced me up and down on its back.

It was growing colder and we had been riding for hours. I had no idea what the time was... or the day...

Ahead was a valley with a few scattered, low-slung houses. My teeth were chattering. I was so hungry and thirsty. Mostly thirsty.

"Please give me something to drink."

McBulbous grunted angrily, rode our horse down the side of the trail, and stopped in a field. The men all dismounted and began urinating at the edge of the clearing. McBulbous reached up and yanked me from the horse. Even though he was doing this every single time I couldn't figure out how to prepare, how to stop my fall. I crashed down on my shoulder again. I screamed up at him from the ground, "You are a fucking monster."

"You have told me this afore."

His shadow loomed over me, big and hulking. Scary. "Well,

it's still true. You haven't done one redeeming thing since I met you." I pulled my tartan tighter around my shoulders. It was freezing out here. "Just an asshole. And I took history classes. We studied all the assholes throughout history and guess what? You're proving yourself to be right up there at the top of the list. Biggest of all time."

He was digging through a sack for something. "Och aye, well ye winna be needin' tae worry about it come shortly, because ye will be on your own."

"Wait—" I glanced around. "You can't leave me here? You can't! I'll die out here. Take me to the houses at least. Then leave me, I'll figure it out from there — oh God. It's cold. You can't leave me." I burst into tears curled around my knees. "You can't leave me. I'll die. I don't want to —

Suddenly down the trail, a dust cloud on the road, galloping horse hooves, coming closer—

The men looked around. Some mounted their horses. The sound of hooves drew closer, thundering, one man drew his sword — over the rise, crashing down the roadside — Magnus. His sword held high, his sound a bellowing, his face enraged. He charged toward us.

All of my captors mounted their horses. They rode to meet Magnus about thirty feet away from me and their blades crashed, clanging and wild. Magnus's blade sliced the air in big arcs. He killed a man in three swings. He swung his horse to the next man, fought him while more surrounded him, their blades clanging in the frozen air. The horses screamed, spinning in circles, trampling.

One man lay still in the dirt. One man was injured on the ground holding his leg. Another man fled on his horse. Magnus dropped to the dirt to fight the last man and McBulbous.

I had to help. I was woozy when I stood, but it was Magnus against two men. McBulbous had his back to me. If I attacked him, grabbed his arms, or knocked him to the ground I would be a helpful teammate. As soon as I grabbed McBulbous's arms though he swung his elbow into my nose knocking me screaming and stumbling to the ground.

But then he decided not to fight anymore. He mounted his horse, urged the injured man to mount too, and they rode away.

My nose was on fire, blood poured down my chin. Cramps were still doubling me over. I was sobbing, fear-anguish-freezing, my husband was still fighting the last man in front of me, and all I could do was scramble from the middle of the battle to keep from being trampled and collapse on the cold ground.

The last man shouted something and lunged for his horse. He mounted it, already at a gallop, and fled the scene.

Magnus reached me in three steps and dropped to his knees, pulling my head into his lap. "Kaitlyn, are ye okay?"

He checked my nose and patted around my stomach, then lifted my skirts to see my legs. "There is blood everywhere."

"I know. I'm on my period, my menstrual cycle—" I had no idea if he knew what I was talking about. "My nose hurts. I have terrible cramps. I'm really thirsty." I turned my face into his kilt, clutched the fabric to my face and cried, desperately.

"Och, aye." He gently pulled me off, laid my head on the ground, and rushed to his horse returning with my backpack.

As he rushed back I managed to croak out. "You have it. I thought you might be — like an apparition or something."

He dropped down and pulled my head back to his lap and unzipped the top of the pack. "Kaitlyn, a man lies dead in front of ye, and I am an apparition?"

He unscrewed the top of our water bottle and held it to my

lips so I could drink. I gulped down most of it, and then turned and spewed water all over the ground, groaning and crying.

Magnus's expression was actually fearful and that scared the hell out of me. "We canna stay here; tis growing verra cold and I have killed a man. Can ye move Kaitlyn?"

"Maybe." I sat up with a heave and then felt woozy. My head spun and I collapsed back down.

Magnus zipped our pack, scooped me into his arms, and raced me, jostling, to his horse. He shoved me up to its back, "Hold on," and mounted behind me. He pulled me around the waist into a sitting position, turned the horse, directed us toward the cluster of small houses and forced the horse into a full gallop. The wind was shockingly cold as it rushed toward me. I huddled over the neck of the horse.

He called in through the window at the first house. A woman came out and answered him in a sharp tone. She gestured down the small path and Magnus turned our horse in that direction and pushed it into another gallop pulling to a stop just at the door.

It was growing twilight, gray, almost dark, and the air was ice cold. I was shivering, fear and pain and temperature conspiring against me. Magnus called in from the front yard and a man appeared and they spoke a short exchange. I was clamped tight trying to keep from shaking to pieces. Magnus slipped from the horse, held up his arms for me, and carried me in a bundle into the house.

There was a woman inside who buzzed around Magnus as he carried me in. There was no bed to offer me, but there was a fire at the end of the large room, another pig, more chickens, a goat — Magnus laid me on the ground in front of the hearth. He wrapped my tartan around my shoulders, and a bit under my head, like a sleeping bag.

"When did ye eat last?"

"I had something this morning, no water though, I really need the pain killer in the backpack. Maybe the vitamins. Some water..."

"Kaitlyn, this is Madame Cunningham. She doesn't speak English, but she has some soup for ye. I needs tae see tae the horse. I'll get ye the backpack." He spoke to the man then turned back to me. "There is a stream nae far, I'll refill the water bottle."

He jumped up, spoke briefly to the woman, and disappeared through the front door.

While he was gone, the woman approached me with a filthy rag making a clucking sound that I understood as, "What the heck happened to you? I mean, it's none of my business, but you should not let people bloody your nose like this." Sadly we had no common language so I couldn't breakdown and tell her about being people-trafficked by my mother-in-law.

She used the dingy, smelly rag to wipe the blood from around my nose. Note to self: wash later with the hand cleaner I brought. She smiled kindly, which I supposed meant, *you're cleaned up now*. And then handed me a ceramic bowl with a bit of broth inside. It had some leaves floating in it, also a few pieces of grain that looked like barley. She gestured for me to sip from the bowl.

I was a little warmer. Barely.

About twenty minutes later, Magnus blew into the room on a frost covered wind. He stamped his feet and blew on his fingers, "Tha I fuar an-diugh," and slung the backpack down beside me. He blocked most of the room with the position of his body and unzipped the pack to fish out my bag of medicine. Then he pulled out the water bottle with the filtration straw. I sat up, unscrewed the lid of the Midol bottle, dropped four pills into my hand, slammed them in, and gulped them down with cold, fresh, delicious, and oh so necessary water.

I hugged the water bottle to my chest.

Magnus's head hung. He reached for my hand. We both sat without speaking.

There was too much to say. The past two days had been too full of drama and fear to put it to words. This wasn't relief so much as a collapse. I could see it in Magnus's eyes. He couldn't talk or hear or think anymore. He had been in an anguish-propelled panicked motion for days and now he was shutting down. I was shutting down.

The woman handed him a bowl of soup, he drank it quickly, and passed it back to her. I shuffled through the backpack for a tampon and a pad that I brought as backups for my new menstrual cup. Well, guess what? I wasn't using the cup here. In this room the tampons and pads were familiar and Plan A. I stood and headed for the chamber pot. It was filthy and reeked of urine.

Luckily it was fairly dark in this corner of the house. Magnus sat at the far end, in the flickering light of the fire, turned away. The older couple huddled in the other far corner, the other side of the fire. I lifted my skirts, pulled down my damp long-underwear, and my soaked-through panties, and peed while I pasted the pad to my panties thinking, *Better late than never,* but adding a question mark to the end, because was it? My skirts were trashed, stained and gross. I wiggled to dry myself and pulled up my underwear, dropped my skirts and returned to the fire. Magnus was leaned on the wall, legs akimbo, hand on his sword. I laid down and put my head on his lap.

I whispered, "Did Lizbeth's husband survive?"

He answered, "Nae."

"Oh. But Sean is alive?"

"Aye, he has lived." His hand was resting beside my head, but then his fingers went into my hair, entwining in it. He took a deep breath and moments later I fell asleep.

～

A few hours later I shifted, then turned to see him looking down at me. "Do you need to lie down?"

"Nae, I need tae be ready..."

"Oh. Okay." I laid my head back down on his lap. A moment later I whispered, "What do you need to be ready for?"

"In case they come back."

CHAPTER 28

The next morning we rose at dawn. It was icy cold crisp outside, but we trudged across the fields towards the stream where we were going to time-journey back to Florida. It was hidden there so we figured we could do it without being seen. I felt a lot better, well enough to journey at least. Ice cream at the end of the trip would fix me right up. The grass was so frosty it crinkled when we stepped on it. Everything shimmered and was so beautiful. I took out my phone and photographed the fields and took a photo of my husband, a sword on his back, big and powerful. In his own natural landscape, wrapped in a plaid. The only thing out of place was the backpack he carried by the straps.

We came to the stream. A large tree to block us from sight. We scanned the area to make sure we were alone. Magnus unzipped the backpack to get the time vessel. I huddled close.

He twisted the middle and absolutely nothing happened. He turned the ends so the markings would appear. No matter what he touched or twisted or pulled, the whole thing lay motionless, unlit, completely dead, defunct.

"It's broken?" I felt the blood rush to my head with panic.

He didn't answer. He kept twisting the dials, harder, angrier, desperately.

"Why won't it start?"

"I daena ken." His voice was like a growl.

"Has it ever done this before?"

"Nae, it has always worked."

"Maybe you aren't—"

"I'm doing it the right way, the same way, tis nae turning on. I will say the numbers." He listed the numbers while we both held the vessel in our hands, but there was nothing happening with it. At all. He twisted again, furiously. Then shoved it back in the pack and and slung the pack over his shoulder. "We are cursed." He stalked across the fields toward the cottage.

"What will we do?"

"We will return to Balloch then I will meet with Lady Mairead."

I was hustling to keep up with his long furious stride.

"You think she will help? I mean, she paid those guys to kidnap me, I—"

He stopped and turned to me. "What did ye say?"

"They said she paid them to take me."

He watched my face closely, then shook his head. He turned and began walking again.

"But maybe she'll give you one of the other vessels?"

"I am nae asking for help, I plan tae kill her."

It was freezing cold, but we needed to get about four hours of distance in the day to get to the next village for the night. We went a different direction, across fields and a small stream, to a path that the farmer had described because Magnus was worried we might be followed or tracked. We were in the middle of the dawn of the eighteenth century, in a forest somewhere Magnus had never been before, miles from the next house, or village, or anything.

We rode in silence.

This was different from the silence of our ride together to Fort Clinch. That trip had been full of sighs and wanting to touch each other. And different still from the silence that first time we came to 1702, a ride full of fury and energetic refusing-to-speak. This silence was full of a big stinking pile of "what to say?" I'm sorry you were kidnapped? Thank you for rescuing me? I'm glad you didn't die. These things were too big to need to be said. But they were piling in a pile so big it threatened to spill over and crush us under.

Magnus's voice shocked me, an hour or so into our ride. The morning was chilled, quiet, still. There was a mist floating around our bodies and the trail. Magnus was sitting straighter, paying attention to the path. "When I found ye, why were the men off their horses?"

"I don't know, I think they were planning to leave me there to die."

He made a tch-tch sound to our horse and made it pick a treacherous path around a large boulder.

"What did they do tae ye?"

"Besides kidnapping, starving, tying up, and being just real assholes, nothing. I mean, if you're wondering if I was raped, no, but it still sucks."

I sat for a second staring ahead of us, down the path, his arms around me but barely touching me.

"And what if I had been raped? What if, Magnus? Would you leave me? Would you hate me? What about your marriage vows, those still matter, you don't get to decide I'm damaged goods—"

His voice rumbled behind my head. "I am asking ye for the story of it, tis all."

Tears filled my eyes. "They didn't do anything. They told me you were dead. They made me believe that no one was coming for me..."

He steered our horse around a fallen tree.

"And they were just taking me as far away as they could get me, to leave me to die somewhere." I burst into tears and folded over the neck of our horse and sobbed for a long long time. Magnus pulled the horse to a stop and sat still, behind me, not touching, while I cried.

Then I recovered myself.

And rose up again.

Brushed the wet hair off my face. "Why are you being so mean?"

The horse wanted to move. It sidestepped, and Magnus passed the reins into both hands and held it still. I felt him take in a deep breath. "Mean?"

"You aren't touching me, barely talking to me. It's like you're mad at me."

"You haena been speaking tae me."

"Yeah, well..." I searched my mind for a reason and returned with, "I was busy feeling sorry for myself."

He urged the horse forward again, his arms around me, still barely touching. He remained quiet behind my head.

After a few moments, I said, "Say something. Say something or I'm going to jump off this horse and run into the woods screaming."

"I canna find the words."

I watched the trail as the horse slowly picked its way along it.

He added, "If I speak I may explode. I want tae kill some-one." He rubbed his right hand up and down briskly to warm it on his tartan-covered thigh. Passed the reign to his left hand and rubbed that thigh. "It is all I can do tae keep it in my chest, bound up inside, so I daena hurt ye farther."

"You want to hurt me?"

"Nae Kaitlyn — what do ye take me for?"

"It's what you said."

"I have one purpose in life, tae keep ye safe, and I haena been able tae do it." His breathing was heavy and fast, like he was keeping on top of a wave of pain.

On the side of our path stood a very tall tree. It soared overhead and its trunk was double the diameter of the rest, but as we grew closer, I could see that it was actually two trees, entwined, very near the base. It must have happened many many years ago. Yet here they were still entangled. Now one. I wondered if I could find them in 2018? If I ever got back to 2018. "You rescued me."

"You were taken. They had plans tae kill ye or worse. I have brought this on your life. I daena deserve ye."

I scowled. "Magnus first off, there is not a person alive at any point in history who would look at you, Scottish warrior, capable of rescuing his wife from five men, and then me, disgraced YouTuber, and think I'm the superior person."

"My point is ye wouldna be in these difficulties. Your life wouldna be in danger. Tis my faults that are causin' your destruction."

"Your faults? You sound suspiciously like someone who is about to say to their wife," I mimicked his low voice, because I was starting to get mad. "'It's not you, it's me,' and then recite a list of reasons why we can't be together anymore. Is that what you're about to do?"

"If I stop time-journeyin' maybe then I can keep ye safe."

"So you want us to stay here in the year 1702?"

"Not us, only me."

I tried to twist around to see his face, but my sides were in so much pain I couldn't turn. "I knew it. I knew you were about to say this bullshit to me. What are you going to do; what's your plan? Wait, this morning, were you going to trick me into going into the future alone with the only time vessel? Or were you going to go with me and then disappear on me in the middle of the night?"

I waited for a moment and when he didn't answer I said, "I disagree vehemently with all those plans. Thank god the vessel isn't working, or you might have accomplished it. Jesus Christ Magnus, think about this. You married me in front of God. You made a vow."

I scowled at the horse's mane. "It's a moot point now, we're stuck in 1702. But what, is your plan to kill Lady Mairead for a working time machine just so you can get rid of me? You know what — I'd like to point out that you're taking me against my will. If you want to desert me or send me away, alone, to what — live alone without you? You're no freaking better than those guys who kidnapped me. Let me off."

He didn't slow the horse.

"Magnus, let me off the horse right now."

"Nae, tis too cold."

"I am not going with you. I will die right here. I might as well. Let me off this godforsaken horse. Right now."

My voice grew so grim he pulled the horse to a stop.

With a huge effort and almost unbearable pain, I swung a leg over and flounced to the ground. It was absolutely freezing. I yanked my tartan tight around my head, tight under my throat. Frosty breath in front of my face.

"Kaitlyn, what are ye doing?"

"I am not riding on a horse with someone who plans to desert me to die all by myself. I won't do it."

"You'll die here, Kaitlyn, tis too cold for ye—"

"I don't care. I'm going to stand here and wait for my husband to come and rescue me. Because that's what he does. He saves my life. He doesn't say bullshit stuff like I'm not going to be married to you anymore because you're better than me, and he sure as hell doesn't plan to desert me. Unlike you. You can just go on your merry way. You wanted to leave me, consider it done."

By now I was shivering pretty noticeably. From the cold, the stress, the shadow of Magnus over me.

From up on the horse Magnus said, "Kaitlyn, you will freeze..."

I stared straight ahead. "I know. But it's worth it to not be on a horse with a kidnapper anymore."

The horse began high-stepping in a circle. Magnus pulled it back in front of me.

"What do you want me tae say?"

I stamped my feet, half-petulantly, half-freezing. "My husband would know what to say."

His face stormed over.

"He would rescue me, then he would hold me in his arms while I cried. And he would tell me he was sorry for all the asinine men of the world. And he would tell me he loved me, and that he would never ever leave me. Until he comes I am not going anywhere."

Magnus glared at me. He spun the horse around and galloped down the path by twenty feet, then yelled, "Hie!" turned the horse and galloped back. He pulled short in front of me. "Kaitlyn, get on the horse."

"No."

"Kaitlyn, I am nae askin' ye, I am tellin' ye, get on the horse."

"Absolutely not."

He swung the horse around. He galloped away, bellowing. He swung back, kicking up a cloud of frosty dust and pulled short in front of me again. He dismounted, dropping in front of me, and stood there for a second, breathing heavily.

I continued to look straight ahead, my view his Adam's apple.

He stood there.

I stood there.

Finally I grabbed him around the chest, buried my face in his tartan, and burst into tears.

He wrapped his arms around.

"Mo reul-iuil." He held me close and tight, his arms around my head, his cheek pressed to my hair.

I nodded, rubbing my tear-stained face up and down on the front of his shirt. "I want to go home."

"I know, mo reul-iuil. I know."

"With you though, I want to go home with you."

"Aye, me too."

I held him harder.

Finally he rumbled, "Tis hard tae come home from battle."

"I know. It is for me too."

"I didn't protect you, I promised."

"I know."

He held me tighter, warmer, closer.

"But it's okay now." I snuffled into his shirt. "It's okay."

I felt him nod against my head, and I knew he was coming back from the battlefield, finally. My hands were wrapped inside my plaid, I reached up and held his cheeks and looked up into his eyes. "We're going to be okay. We'll do what Barbara always says to do, 'Begin each day where you are.' We have to begin. We have to get home. And we have to do it together."

"I have tae get ye to a warm house."

I hugged him, my body fully shivering now.

"I need ye tae ride behind me and hold on, so we can go fast."

CHAPTER 29

$\mathcal{W}$e pulled up to another cottage and Magnus dismounted from the horse to inquire inside. We were advised to ride down a field to another house, because as Magnus put it, "The house was so full of bairns, I canna imagine they have a floorboard tae spare."

The next house was much like the others — an older couple lived there, with more animals than it seemed wise to keep in a small space. It smelled horrific. They gave us a spot near the fire, but seemed irritated by our presence.

While Magnus went out to see to our horse, the woman of the house bustled around me, cranky and fitful. She hovered, working near the fire, where I was perched on a tiny stool. She didn't want me there, but I didn't want to give up my spot. I needed it, plus Magnus had arranged for me to sit here. I accidentally bumped her elbow which irritated her further.

She seemed to think I was a massive inconvenience. I felt it too but I couldn't even imagine how to help. There was one pot and filth everywhere but I had no experience with cleaning pig sties in the eighteenth century.

Magnus returned. He and I sat on small stools without much to do but warm by the fire. Magnus held my hand. Then he leaned forward into my lap, wrapping around my arm. His forehead on my shoulder. I bowed my head so I could hear his words.

"Our lives, mo reul-iuil are full of too many apologies. I daena believe I would have left ye, I would have stopped myself, surely, but I have spent many a long hour in the past days thinking ye would be better without me."

"You cannot think it without meaning something so awful I can't even bear it Magnus. I am not better without you. Because we're together now, entwined and entangled, like that tree today in the woods. There isn't any going back." The warmth of the fire popping and crackling in the fireplace spread only about five feet away but we were within the circumference of the heat. Almost comfortable for the first time all day. And the warmth was spreading into my body, coursing through my blood, warming my heart. The anger from earlier, at the predicament, at his reaction, at my past few days, began to dissipate.

Magnus was doing the best he could. This was all so complicated and he had done so much. He had to fight back from the battle and now he had to rationalize back into my arms.

He needed help.

I pressed my lips to his forehead. "Did you mean it when you said we were cursed?"

"Och, aye."

"Did it ever occur to you that the path you are on, coming forward in time — to me, might be a part of God's plan? Why do you think you're going against him?"

His forehead grew heavier on my shoulder. "I daena ken."

"Exactly." I whispered into his ear. "You don't know. God has never spoken to you outright. You pray to him all the time, but he doesn't answer, not directly. So how do you know? Maybe it's God's plan for you to come to the Island in 2017 and meet me.

Maybe we're supposed to get married and have children. Maybe you have a genetic purpose or—"

"Genetic?"

"Like your bloodline, your children."

"Maybe our bairns are a part of God's plan?"

"Maybe. The truth is you don't know. All you can do is try to live and be good. And I think you are. You didn't plan to do any of this. You didn't build the time vessel. You didn't come to Florida to do anything wrong. You aren't building an army, or transporting guns, or conspiring to take over the world. You're literally just trying to keep the vessels from falling into the hands of someone who wants to do bad things with them."

He raised up slightly to see my face. His brow drawn, listening.

"And you're keeping your vows. I think that means the most to God."

"Perhaps I haena displeased him?"

I shrugged. "You can't know."

"You are right, I canna know." He stared deep into my eyes, then asked, "Would ye pray with me Kaitlyn?"

I nodded.

He knelt on the floor beside his stool and I knelt beside him, shoulder to shoulder. And he began to pray, murmuring, in words I didn't understand, his voice low and rumbling in the room.

And though I hadn't prayed in a very long time, I said my own. I prayed to keep him safe, to keep him strong and sure. And I didn't ask to go home. That seemed too much like bargaining, and possibly impossible, but instead I asked for guidance wherever I was.

When we were done we stood and he kissed me on my temple. And then pulled me into his arms and held me for a long long time. The anger, the fear, the anguish, all left him and he had returned to the kind of strength we needed to get through this together.

~

When our focus returned to the room we were in, the woman of the house seemed satisfied by our prayer.

She drew Magnus into a conversation, speaking long and sharply about a great many angry things. Her husband grunted in reply, but only when he had to, but she was all exasperated expressions and furious gestures. I had no idea what she was talking about, but it was much like she was saying, "kids these days, with their gyrating and rock-and-roll," or, "the neighbors with their fornicating ways."

Magnus placated her as well as he could, saying something that sounded a lot like it meant, "Yes ma'am, I agree with absolutely everything you say." When her back was turned, he gave me a sad smile with a shake of his head and I crossed my eyes and stuck out my tongue in return.

Finally, she gave us a thick soup for dinner. We shared a beer. As I fell asleep in Magnus's arms he whispered, "I could tell she was a judging ye as nae godly enough. Thank ye for praying with me." and I was reminded that my husband had been looking out for me, always. And would for all time. Definitely. "I will get you home, mo reul-iuil. I promise."

CHAPTER 30

The next afternoon we arrived at Balloch and headed straight for the Great Hall though I was a complete wreck. My hair had dreadlocks in the back, my eyes were tinged black, my clothes were stained. I stunk too, plain and simple.

Magnus was soon in a conversation with a group of men about rescuing me. And I stood to the side, unnecessary.

Lizbeth rushed in once she heard we were there and hugged me like a long-lost sister.

I said, "I am so sorry about your husband." We sank onto a bench holding hands. "I tried to save him." Her head was bowed. "I tried to comfort him as he died. I'm just so sorry Lizbeth."

"Thank you, Kaitlyn." She pushed her hair back from her forehead. Her eyes were swollen from tears, her face pale. "He was a terrible husband in many ways, but he was my own, and kept me from the trouble of gettin' another." She sounded a lot like her mother, Lady Mairead.

She waved her hand of my worry. "You have been through an ordeal, what has happened tae ye?"

"These men grabbed me and stole me from the battlefield. They took me really far away and—" I burst into tears.

"Did they hurt ye Kaitlyn?"

"No, not really. It was just so scary. They told me Magnus was dead, and I just — thought that was the end of it for me."

Lizbeth clucked, not in a mean way but in a there, there way. She pushed my hair from my wet cheek.

"You daena have an end tae ye, because ye are a part of my family now. You are a Campbell, the wife of Young Magnus, the sister of Lizbeth and Sean. The niece of the Earl. Your family resides in Argyll most of the time. Have ye seen it yet sister, our home there?"

"I haven't."

"It is beautiful on the edge of Loch Awe. I miss it greatly. But now we are here under the Earl of Breadalbane's protection in Balloch Castle on the south bank of the Tay, and we have great power, Kaitlyn. You are protected by us."

I nodded and swallowed down my tears.

"Did Young Magnus kill your captors?"

"He killed one of them, the rest escaped."

"He must be regrettin' going alone. Sean would have gone with him gladly. But tis nae matter, ye are home. I will need ye tae attend me during the wake. I have taken a break, but must go back. You will needs be cleaned up before ye come."

"How, I don't have any more clothes?"

"I will send someone with ye and a dress to change." She stood and spoke with one of the young women milling about the room. Then she whispered to Magnus and soon I was ushered upstairs to my room to change.

CHAPTER 31

*a*n hour later I was shown to the family chapel. It was a small room, but with ceilings that swept very high, and two long stained glass windows. Tapestries and paintings along the sides. Near the altar stood two heavy oak tables and in the middle of one lay Lizbeth's husband, Rory.

He looked scrubbed, his clothes clean. A shield on his chest. A sword beside him. I winced when I saw him, remembering pressing the cloth to his wound, trying to keep him alive. Maybe if I hadn't been kidnapped I could have saved him, but then again first aid might not have been enough and there was no hospital.

On the other table lay another shield and sword upon a body that was covered over in a cloth.

Lizbeth gestured to sit on the bench beside her. She whispered, "There lies Ewan. The Earl was able tae recover his body."

"Oh." I gulped trying to push down a feeling of panic. Images flashed in my head: Ewan's forearm across my throat. My husband beating him nearly to death. Ewan's struggle as his throat was cut. I wanted to run from the room. I closed my eyes and alternately stared at my hands in my lap, anywhere but the front of the room.

On my other side sat a very young woman who gave me a small prim nod. And we sat there in front of the two bodies. I thought about all the women through history who had done this, watching over dead husbands. All the sadness and tragedy and loss, but also, as in the case of Lizbeth, the beginning of a hard scramble again — to find a new warrior and protector. And how it had always been the same.

Until finally changing in my lifetime into something else. Where a bereaved widow could say, "I don't need anyone, I can be on my own." But then *oh* to never have anyone call you mo reul-iuil again. No one to whisper in foreign tongues into your ear. And yes, I spent a long time in that chapel thinking about how close I came to losing Magnus...

CHAPTER 32

*L*ater Lizbeth and I returned to the Great Hall for dinner and beer. She asked, "What do you think of your other sister, Maggie, Sean's wife?"

"Is that who that was? I hadn't met her yet."

"She will be most of the time at the wake, or with the babies in the nursery. When she is with us, she will keep her eyes cast down. She is pious and godly and I'm grateful for her every day because she might be our family's one chance tae redeem ourselves before God. I am certain he will be a'holdin my mother against us."

Magnus and the other men were in high spirits and looked quite drunk. Sean kissed and hugged me hello and made many remarks about the bruises around my eyes. Magnus pulled me aside for a moment, his hands on my waist, pulling me close to his front. "I am sorry mo reul-iuil, I tried the vessel again today. Tis nae working.

"What are we going to do?"

"I daena know, I will keep tryin'. Tomorrow is the burial. I want ye tae know, ye are nae invited."

"Why not?"

"Women daena go tae burials, tis unseemly." He grinned at my shock.

"Not even Lizbeth?"

He shook his head. "She is expected to sit here and think long on her husband. I imagine she will keep ye company with jokes and merry stories. I am expected tae go."

It made me a little panicky. "How far away will you be, I mean, not far, right? I don't — I wish we had a phone."

"Nae far and I will leave orders that one of the boys will ride tae me if something is wrong."

I nodded. I could see in his eyes that this was the best he could do. He couldn't skip the funeral to stay with the women. It was his brother-in-law they were burying after all, his cousin.

He pulled me into his arms and kissed my forehead. "Begin where we are?"

"Begin where we are," I agreed.

We sat at a long table and listened to long stories about battles fought. Most of the words I barely understood but there was a great deal of miming that went along with it. I understood even more as I drank. There was a lot of laughing and Magnus held my hand.

I tried to put my fear and worry away. I was stuck, but not for long. Magnus would fix this. I needed to find comfort in the simple things, like being a part of his family, here in his house, safe, fed and tipsy, kissed on my forehead by him, part of him, entwined.

The following day Lizbeth and I sat in the nursery with her children, Jamie, who was four years old, and Mary, who was two. Maggie was there with her son, Gavin, who was one years old.

There were also lots of other women and children. We played with the kids a bit. I taught them the Itsy Bitsy Spider nursery rhyme, possibly ruining forever the entire history of the world. And then for fun I taught them how to do the dance that goes with the song, YMCA. Everyone laughed, though Maggie demurely covered her mouth and seemed a little shocked by it all.

Then I told them about funny animals I had seen, usually on video or memes, but changing the story so that it was, 'An animal I saw did this...' Until Lizbeth, laughing, said, "There are so many animals where ye are from. I would love tae go see it someday. When ye have a baby, Kaitlyn, we'll come to visit. Maggie and I will make Sean take us. What would it take tae get tae the New World?"

"God, like months I would think! It's so far away, better let me come to see you."

I told her about my house on the Island and about chef Zach, and that was how we whiled away the time. Me regaling her with stories about my life, but with almost every single word changed. Sometimes I sounded really bizarre stuttering and correcting myself so much.

The men returned. Their mood even more jovial than the night before. The Great Hall was full to capacity and really truly warm for once. Bagpipers played and men danced and sang. Some stood and told long sweeping stories, and the audience cheered and banged their cups. Lizbeth, the wife, was mostly inconsequential sitting off to the side. She had shared his bed, but the men who shared the battlefield got the floor, the memories, the pats on the back.

A man, who looked to be about thirty and pretty handsome for this crowd, stood and said something loud and boisterous. The men cheered and as he was about to sit down, he raised his glass in Lizbeth's direction.

"Who's that?"

She blushed. "That is Liam. He is the husband I have been wantin' for long years, but he has been married tae my cousin. He broke me heart quite soundly."

"Oh, wow, where is she?"

"She died last year in childbirth."

My eyes went wide.

She whispered, "And he has nae found another wife."

And you're widowed, and he's widowererered." I giggled having trouble getting the words out. "I'm tipsy. You're widowered. I mean, he's widowerered. You're both alone. You might have a chance with him." When I followed her eyes she was watching Liam across the tables. He glanced up and met her eyes.

He was smaller than Magnus, dark haired, not as handsome, but the way he spoke and everyone laughed, he seemed to be the life of the party.

"Is he smart, brave, kind, all the good stuff?" I hiccuped.

"Aye, he's all of that and more."

"Girlfriend you are in deep." I giggled even harder.

Magnus sat beside me. "What are ye talking of?" He saw the blush on Lizbeth's cheeks and followed her view across the table to the opposite end to Liam. He chuckled. "You still have a thought for him? I thought ye were mourning your husband today, sister. I am thinkin' ye may well be a wicked woman."

"You know as well as I, young Magnus, that my husband, as much as I be a missin' him, was nae a good husband, though I would never admit it at his funeral because I am nae wicked, just a realist. I will need a husband fast tae take care of me and the children."

"You know Sean and I will protect ye."

"I know ye will," she patted the back of his hand. "But a husband, as your wife will attest, is more than just protection. If he is a good husband, he is an ally and a warm bed."

Magnus said, "Aye sister, but be wise this time and marry him afore ye take him tae bed. Twas a difficult arrangement tae strike last time."

"Shush young Magnus or your wife will think me a harlot."

I shook my head and grinned. "Not at all Lizbeth. My grandmother used to say, 'You can't judge another woman for the deals she strikes with her lovers.'"

Lizbeth grinned. "Oh, I like my new sister so much. Ye will keep her here, so she can be a part of us?"

"I wish I could Lizbeth, but I have made her a promise tae take her home."

"Nae too soon, I hope?"

"As soon as I can."

Lizbeth was looking from one of us to the other. Then she pouted, "But I was hoping that Kaitlyn would be able tae help me with my finding of a husband."

"I wish I could. It is one of my favorite pastimes and I hate to miss you doing the conquering, because that man over there — he looks like you'll have fun climbing him to the summit."

Magnus and Lizbeth laughed so hard that everyone turned to look down at our end of the table. Magnus waved them away.

Sean slid into the bench seat beside us. "What's this?"

Magnus said, "Your sister is eyeing Liam, and my wife is telling her tae be cautious and godly."

We all cracked up.

Sean said, "Are ye now? Tis very pious of ye, but ye might be speaking tae the wind, Kaitlyn. I'm sure ye have heard Lizbeth's tale of wifely woe, most the other women are hoping she will marry again so they can stop the hearing of it." Lizbeth swatted him on the arm indignantly.

I said, "I don't mind hearing her tell of wifely woes, but I prefer to hear the sordid tales of conquest."

Sean laughed. "Now see Magnus, I have told ye tae marry a demure godly young woman. Someone who will perform her wifely duties and spend the rest of the time in prayer so ye can have some peace. But here ye are, marrying someone too much alike your sister, with her sharp mind and mouth ye winna have much peace."

Magnus raised his glass. "Tis nae my style, I like a woman with a better wit."

Sean waved him away with a hand. "You learned it in London. Ye will be your own man though I tried tae be a guide for ye."

Lizbeth laughed a sparkling laugh. "You won't find young Magnus wanting anything tae do with a woman like Maggie, he would be bored out of his mind in a day. I think Kaitlyn suits him just fine. But they are leaving soon Sean, and what am I tae do? I will have tae resort tae spending my day sewing with Maggie in a nursery full of bawling bairns."

Sean asked, "You are leaving us Magnus?"

"Och aye. I need tae get Kaitlyn home safe."

"I'll be sure tae tell mother ye send your best wishes." Sean smiled and swigged from his beer.

Magnus growled, "If you see Lady Mairead before I do, ye shall tell her I am coming tae hold her to account."

Lizbeth laughed, "Magnus ye sound so malevolent!"

Sean said, "He thinks Lady Mairead paid the men who abducted Kaitlyn."

Magnus said, "I daena think it, I know it."

Lizbeth said, "Oh no, really? That mother of ours is diabolical. I have just been tellin' Kaitlyn that our family will always have her protection as our own and now this." She leaned for my arm. "I am sorry for it, sister, our mother is—"

"Not to be trusted." I finished for her.

She laughed. "I was going to say, a wicked witch of a woman, but yes, you can't trust her either. But why? Why does she want tae do ye harm?"

"I don't really know. She asked me to keep Magnus with me on the Island. She had me sign a contract for it, but keeping my husband bound when he needed to come back here really wasn't something I could do."

"You signed a contract with my mum?"

I nodded.

Magnus said, "Twas before I could warn her. She forced Kaitlyn tae marry me."

"Forced? I daena ken young Magnus, I have seen the way your wife looks at ye, tis nae a matter of forcing."

"Not at all," I dipped my head to his shoulder.

"It daena make sense why she wants tae keep ye from here, from your home. What are ye goin' tae do?"

"Take Kaitlyn home, so she is away from Lady Mairead."

Lizbeth nodded. "Makes more sense now I ken the meaning of it. Fine, better a safe sister than one here being abused and maligned by our mother, but tis time tae take Lady Mairead in hand. She has been a blight on us for far too long."

Both the men agreed. Then, as the night had been long and there had been a lot of drinking, it was time to stumble up the stairs to our room.

CHAPTER 33

*I*n the light of a cold morning I woke, my head and arms sprawled across Magnus's chest. I looked up to see his eyes open. He nudged me up.

"My head hurts," I said, "that was a lot of drinking last night."

"Och aye, drinking at a funeral must be done with more commitment than other times as a sign of respect."

I yawned loud and long and rolled onto my stomach, my chin on his chest. "Funerals really get ya thinking, don't they?"

"What do ye mean?"

"Makes me wonder how I would carry on without the people I love. How I'll carry on without my grandmother, for instance, and what if she died without me being there? What if the last thing she knows of me is me dropping her off at the nursing home?"

"Tis why we are takin' ye home."

"Us, why we're taking us home."

"Aye."

"Promise?"

"I promise, I haena a thought of living without ye Kaitlyn. I daena ken what I had about me afore, but tis nae a thought anymore." He wrapped his arms around me.

Muffled in his arms I said, "Okay. Good." I thought for a moment, the bleary thoughts of a hung-over woman. "I think I saw her at Talsworth during the battle, up on the... What is that called, the high wall?"

Magnus raised his head. "The high wall, the one above the field? You think you saw Lady Mairead, was she watching?"

"Yes, I think it was her. I noticed her just before I was..."

Magnus took a deep breath and blew it out. "I will have tae go get a vessel from her."

I traced a circle on his chest with my finger.

"That sounds scary and dangerous and—"

A very faint buzzing sound met my ears.

"Do you hear that?"

Magnus raised up on one arm, shaking me off, looking around the floor of the room. "My sporran, the vessel..." He leapt from the bed with nothing on, and man, what a majestic ass. Like really, the kind of ass sculptors would want to carve and it was all mine. Mine mine mine.

He shoveled through the pile of heavy clothes on the floor and pulled his sporran up, opened the top and pulled out the vessel.

"It's working?"

"Aye," he twisted the dials through the middle and it buzzed to life.

Relief washed over me. "But not yet, turn it off Magnus. You're naked and we need to say goodbye to Lizbeth first."

He turned the dial so that the vessel turned off again and continued looking down at it.

I jumped off the bed to the ice cold floor and picked up my dress. "Imagine if we disappeared from our room without saying goodbye. Everyone would be so freaked out." I stopped when I realized he was still looking down at the vessel. "What?"

He said, "It has never turned on like this afore."

"Oh." I scurried across the cold floor to our chamber pot. I crouched and peed with relief. My period was done, the vessel was working, this was going to be a good day.

"It's probably nothing. I mean, it also never stopped working before, and now — maybe it's just shorting out or something..." My voice trailed off because that was an awful thought. How safe was time-jumping with a wonky vessel?

"Shorting out?"

"Like the energy that makes it work is having trouble getting to all the parts to — you know, let's forget I said anything."

"Aye, tis nae making it better."

I returned to the bed, stepped into my skirts, and pulled them up. "The truth is, we don't know how it works. We're kind of stuck using it without knowing and hoping for the best."

Magnus nodded and stuffed it in his sporran.

"When should we go?"

"Today I think, if Lady Mairead is at Talsworth. Tis only a few hours away, I daena think Balloch is safe."

I wrestled the bodice over my arms and head, groaning in pain because my middle was still pretty sore, and turned so Magnus could do my laces. I said, "We also know she has two vessels. I'm worried the Island isn't safe because she knows where we live."

"Och aye, I have been thinkin' on it and she will follow us."

"Plus, I think she has a way of knowing where we are. There is probably a tracer or tracker on the vessel. Don't you think? When I arrived in 2017, she came and met me."

"You think so?"

I nodded.

He cinched the laces tight and tied them.

"You're getting good at this."

The corner of his mouth curled up, "I would prefer to be practicing the undressin'."

"My period is over so that's good news."

"Tis usually the time the men of my clan would go on a hunt."

"Really? Men would plan a hunt to get away from their wives when they're menstruating?"

He chuckled. "And their mothers and their sisters and their cousins. And then when they came home from the hunt they would blame the women for everything that went wrong."

"That is insane."

"I daena think on it much afore, but tis nae sensible. You canna kill the crops with a look."

I rolled my eyes. "That's so forward thinking of you."

He chuckled but then his brow furrowed, "Maybe I need tae speak with her."

I shook my head. "No, I don't think... what if we went back but instead of the Island, what if we went to Los Angeles or something? We could put the vessel into a vault at the bank and then we could hide in the crowds for a while. We could call Chef Zach and tell him we're home. We'd have access to our money. There would be no way for Lady Mairead to find us in Los Angeles."

"I found ye."

"We won't tweet our location this time."

"I know ye daena want tae hear it, but I must say it. I think I will have tae come back, we canna hide forever."

I put my hands on his cheeks and looked into his eyes. I pushed a lock of his hair off his forehead. "I know. I know it in my heart Magnus. I do. But right now I want to go home. I want you to come home. I want Chef Zach to cook for us. I want to see Baby Ben. I want to walk on the beach with you. I just — I know it. I just want us to have a few days of normal before you run off fighting again."

His strong arms wrapped around my middle and lifted me into a big, leave-the-ground, hug. He nestled his face into my shoulder and said into my skin, where it passed through my cells into my center being, "Aye, mo reul-iuil, we are going home."

CHAPTER 34

The day was the warmest I had ever experienced in Scotland, like a balmy 55 degrees. The sky was blue and my entire opinion of Scotland changed. The landscape was beautiful. The castle against the sky. The deep green of the grass. The craggy stones, and wispy clouds overhead. We had no battles planned, no dramas to deal with right now. Only the "soon" to confront Lady Mairead, but not now. Now was for walking into the woods to go home. We shared a big meal with Magnus's family, laughing and talking. We went to the nursery to say goodbye to the nieces and nephews and spoke with the Earl about our plans to go and when we planned to return. On every count we tried to be vague.

We walked from the castle without taking a horse, hoping we confused everyone enough that no one questioned why we didn't take a horse and where we were actually going after all.

All we had to do was get to the woods.

We held hands as we walked and Magnus told me about the trees, the river, his childhood living here. I had seen the nursery with little Jamie toddling around in it. It was easy now to imagine Magnus toddling around in his childhood home. Warmth flooded my body at the idea of him, young and child-like, growing up here, protected. Sun on my skin, a sweet sort of laughter at something funny he said, his palm clutched to mine. We came to a bright, sun-filled clearing, and my husband pulled me to his front, reached around, and grabbed my bottom.

"Och, I have missed this arse, is it under there somewhere?" He began lifting my skirts in big bunched handfuls until he got them up enough to put a big strong palm on each bare butt cheek. With a chuckle, he said, "I knew twas there, just had tae work for it." He pulled me closer, bent down, his breath hot on my shoulder between my throat and my wool.

"If you can wait dear sir, until Florida, I can take all these clothes off and show you proper."

He chuckled again. "Twill take too long, Madame. We have a journey. Then all these laces. I winna be able to wait."

I pressed my full skirts against his bundle of wrapped kilt and yes — "I see, you want me."

"Och aye, mo reul-iuil, wrap your arms."

I wrapped my arms around his neck and he lifted me from the ground. I wrapped my legs around his back, so much fabric between us that it was quite comical how heavy I was and how much struggling it took. He prepared to crouch to the ground with me in his arms. "Be careful Magnus — everything hurts."

"I will be gentle." He lowered me to my back, very carefully, on the grassy ground.

"Especially my ribs and right here." I gestured around my whole stomach area.

He chuckled against my neck. "We only need one part for this." His voice had gone deep, full, primal. He raised up to his knees and pushed the front of my skirts to my waist and adjusted his tartan from his front while I took in the sight of him, Magnus, warrior, Scottish, in his woods, wanting me so bad he had dropped me to the ground.

I was so freaking hot for him. He climbed on me, and, oh god, in me, and my legs wrapped around him as he drove against me long, and deep and slow. Mostly clothed, wool and spice and warm grass and the smells of the woods. It was new for us, to be outside, taking our time. Super sexy to want to touch him everywhere but only touching in that one sweet sweet space.

We spent a long time, making it last, kissing and slowing, groaning and moaning into each other's ears. Until finally we ended, having used up all our patience and control in gentleness and care and with a final fast fury he collapsed on my body, spent and relaxed. His breaths fast and then deepening, he slid from me, now inconsequential.

"Twas okay, I dinna hurt ye?"

"No that was awesome."

"I have been needin' ye, what has it been five days, mo reul-iuil?"

"In my time it felt like months." I kissed his cheek. "Usually there's plenty to do during my period, but I felt about as unsexy as could be between the kidnapping and the filthy clothes."

He kissed down my neck and kissed my chest. I drew in a breath, my skin rising to meet his lips. "You are sexy just fine."

I drew my fingertips down his cheek. "You sir, have a very good imagination."

His cheek rested on my chest. "I remember ye in the shower, tis true, and in your tiny little dress, the blue one with the flowers?"

"You like that dress?"

"Verra much. When ye bend it goes verra short, tis a fine arse, mo reul-iuil."

I giggled, causing his head to shake with my jiggling breasts.

"Are we going to stay here all day? I hate to say it but we should get home soon."

Magnus heaved himself up and off me. "What are we going tae ask Chef Zach tae make us for dinner?"

"I want a burger with five toppings. I don't care what they are, but five. And those buns that are so fat and greasy and browned that they taste like they've been cooked in butter? Plus, French fries. Three different kinds. Long and skinny and crispy, the ones like planks with potatoey goodness inside, and tater tots with too much salt. Lastly, a salad. I don't know if I'll eat it, I might just want it on my plate because I could eat it if I wanted to."

Magnus adjusted the folds of his kilt. "You have given it a great deal of thought. I daena know half of it but sounds delicious and ye may order for us both."

I adjusted my skirts over my legs. "I'll ask him for vanilla ice cream of course, but also, chocolate with chocolate chunks for me."

He looked down at me, still on the ground. "You want tae stand up or sit down for the journey?"

"Let's sit down again. I think your lap is the only way this is going to happen, even with the idea of the French fries in my future."

He sat on the ground and pulled the vessel from his sporran. He turned the dial and it whirred to life.

"It's working?"

"Perfectly."

I stepped a foot on both sides of his thighs and sat on his lap. I curled against him, my cheek pressed to his chest, my arms around his waist, my eyes closed.

"Mo reul-iuil, I will see ye in Florida."

"I love you—"

CHAPTER 35

*I*t is so hard to describe the pain. Pulled apart on a particle level, a nano-particle level, a microscopic, genetic, soul level. The screams in my ears weren't from my mouth, they were from my brain, my cells, my blood boiling, my acids eating through—and then it changed to worse. I had been flung, propelled forward, like through one of those play doh extruders; my body ripped, compressed, torn and shoved, but in one direction. Suddenly I was pulled from around my middle away. The switch hurt. The screaming was real. My body stretched, pulled, my hands grasping air, emptiness. I lost — Magnus. My mind. And then finally, gratefully, consciousness.

Stop screaming. Stop screaming. Stop screaming. Pant pant pant. Open your eyes Kaitlyn, open your goddamn eyes, right now, right now. Right. Now. The ground was stone. The opposite wall looked stone though it was hard to see in the darkness. My breaths were loud. I had been growing used to the sounds of my breaths, able to overcome the strange overly loud noises, but it was back with the pain, the exhaustion, the horror. I was panting as I rode the waves of pain. I shushed myself, shush, shush, shut the fuck up Kaitlyn. Shut. Up. I bit my lips as I writhed in agony. And panted some more.

Where was Magnus? I forced my eyes open and looked around. There was no one with me — a very small room with a wooden door and no furniture. If my mind wasn't tricking me I was in a prison cell. From the looks of the stone, I was in Magnus's time, not my own. There was a window but no light coming through and it was cold, growing colder as the red hot fever pain subsided to be replaced by chills and agony.

Shit.

This was not good.

Two guards walked in, they were sneering and condescending, and frankly pretty abusive with the way they handled me. I had been sleeping and had been, off and on, for hours. It was light outside now and I tried to remember if it had been before or since, and how long I had been in here. There had been two bowls of food passed to me through the door, at intervals. How many hours apart? The men startled me awake, yanked me up without ceremony, and shoved me so hard I fell to a knee.

I blinked away tears as a claw-like grip held my arm. It dragged me down the hallway. I struggled, but it just caused more pain.

"Where are you taking me?"

Silence.

"I demand to know. Where's Magnus Campbell?"

More silence.

The two burley men pushed me up a staircase and down a

hallway and shoved me into a large, ornate, high-ceilinged, exquisitely decorated room. Paintings covered the walls, sculptures filled the floor. A sweeping ceiling with a painting of some kind, Cupids or something overhead. The furniture was lavish, but I didn't have time to gawk. Because at the end of the room sat Lady Mairead, her head tilted, her brow arched at the sight of me. With a languid hand she gestured the guards to bring me forward. Then she smoothed her skirt as, with a shove, they set me in motion.

They deposited me, outraged, in front of her. "Where is Magnus?"

Her head tilted in the other direction. "Ah, Kaitlyn, so good of ye tae come and see me."

"I didn't, I have been kidnapped, more than once. Where am I, and where is Magnus—"

With a small gesture from Lady Mairead the guard to my right knocked me on the side of the head with his fist. I shrieked and fell to my hands and knees.

"And stay down," she commanded.

The guard on my left, yanked me to kneeling. I was holding my sore head, tears streaming down my face.

"Now, we are going tae talk."

I sniffled. The carpet was ornately woven and looked in turns ancient but also brand new. It all looked very different from my last visit to Talsworth so I wasn't sure this was the same place. "Where are we?"

"My husband's castle, Talsworth. Ye will remember your visit. I have been shopping since then, redecorating."

"You've been journeying through time stealing all of this?"

"I am a collector. Nae a thief." She waved it away. "We have business, I think."

I shook my head. "I don't have any business with you."

"You think nae? Tis a pity, I am beginning tae rather like ye."

"What are you even taking about?"

"I have decided the time has come for us tae become conspirators rather than enemies. We should have an interest in forming an alliance."

"Again, still don't know what you're talking about, and no, one contract with an evil person is plenty, thank you."

She squinted her eyes. "I believe that contract you signed with me worked out quite well for ye. You have wealth, a warrior, and a warm bed with young Magnus?" Her eyes were intent on my face. "Daena ye?"

I said, "Yes, but—"

She cut me off with an exasperated tone and said something I didn't understand to the guards. One left my side and Lady Mairead sat quietly. Her gaze sometimes off in the distance, sometimes on my face.

My knees were killing me on the cold stone ground even with the rug and my wool skirts. I dropped lower. "What are you going to do with me?"

"You will be quiet, daena move, and wait. Another word out of ye, another movement, and you will receive another blow."

I stared down at my trembling hands in my lap.

The doors behind me swung open and feet marched down the room. I turned to look over my shoulder but remembered in time Lady Mairead's warning. It sounded like ten men at least.

Then, thrown to the ground and wrestled to his knees — Magnus. He was only ten feet away. His arms bound, shirtless. He struggled against the men who held him, and his face, oh god, his face — beaten to a pulp. His eyes blackened, swollen closed. His nose crooked. His lips swollen and cracked. He turned his head up to look at me, down his nose, through the one part of his eyes that was still able to open, then he stopped struggling against the men holding him still.

"I have explained tae Kaitlyn that she is nae tae move or speak out of turn. Tis the same for you Magnus. I winna suffer ye tae ignore me on this point."

She went to a small table and shuffled through a few papers. A few were on yellow legal pad pages and it sent a chill down my spine. She opened a drawer and rifled through it then returned to her seat. In her hand she held a metal ring about the diameter of a small can, the metal was thick and silvery white. The other ring was thicker, shiny gold, and was about the diameter of a bangle bracelet. She loosely held the silver ring in her left hand and her fingers twisted and fidgeted with the gold ring in her right hand. The whole time her gaze was on Magnus. As if she was mocking him with the items. Though I had no idea what they were.

"You have turned intae a fine warrior, Magnus."

He spit blood from his mouth onto the carpet.

She sneered. Shook her head, then sighed.

"My husband, Delapointe, would like ye dead, Magnus. Lucky for ye tae have someone tae watch over ye."

Magnus growled, "Who?"

"Your father."

Magnus struggled against the men holding his arms. "My father is dead."

"Tis nae true. He is alive. He has heard of your exploits and looks forward tae meeting ye. I am verra proud that ye have gained his favor. Tis what I have dreamed of."

"I will never do anythin' for ye again."

She slowly, languidly appraised him.

"I am sorry tae hear ye say it, Magnus. Our fortunes rely heavily on ye cooperatin' with me."

He struggled and yanked on the ropes and Lady Mairead

said, "Make him stop." Two guards pummeled him, kicking and punching him over and over till he was in a pile on the ground.

I begged, "Stop it, please, stop it. Don't hurt him. Please."

Lady Mairead seemed amused by my pleading. Her lips turned up in a smile.

She said, "Nae more," to the guards, who yanked him up to a kneeling position.

She turned to me. "I dinna say ye could speak, daughter."

"Please don't hurt him anymore."

"Now see, this is what I've been trying to get from you. An understanding of the dire circumstances that might befall your husband. You want tae keep him safe? I suggest ye listen tae what I tell ye tae do."

"Okay." My voice sounded like a whimper and I didn't like it one bit. I tried raising my chest and my chin so I looked more imperial while my knees bruised on the floor.

Lady Mairead sat quietly. She had perfected 'choosing her words carefully.' She spoke slowly and methodically then made us wait.

Magnus's voice erupted in a growl, "You gave payment tae the men tae kidnap Kaitlyn and I will have ye—"

With a flick of her wrist she had her guards bear down on his body again. His groans as they beat him were unbearable. My hands traveled to my ears without knowing they were moving, trying to make a barrier against the onslaught. "Please, you're his mother."

"Och aye, tis why he is still alive. I will be needin' my strong son in the future." She waved her hand and the guards ceased their actions jerking Magnus to his knees once more. "Tis nae tae kill him, tis tae build his strength. I need him strong."

She sighed. "I also need him tae understand I expect him tae submit tae me."

He spit another mouthful of blood to her carpet. "Never."

She leveled her gaze. "See that is where ye are wrong." She cocked her head to the side and her lips turned up at the corner. "But I daena need ye tae make a deal with me."

"Good because I winna."

"I see that. You are covered in blood and in a verra testy mood. Tis a shame, I would have liked tae be more civilized. But Kaitlyn there, she, I believe, is ready tae strike a bargain. So ye arna necessary at all."

To the guards she said, "Take him away, we are through discussing."

Four men yanked him up by the arms and struggled him out of the room. His eyes, closed, bruised, damaged, faced toward me, or near me, sort of at the empty space just above my shoulder and he commanded, "Daena make any deals, Kaitlyn." He was dragged to the end of the room to the door, yelling over his shoulder. "Daena agree with her, daena do it."

The double doors slammed shut and the room went quiet.

"Your husband has given ye an order. This should be fun."

"Why are you such a cold-hearted bitch?"

Lady Mairead took in a deep breath. "Tis what ye think of me, daughter?"

"Yes, one hundred percent. Without a doubt. Given some thought I could probably come up with worse names, but cold-hearted bitch rings perfectly true." I shifted my weight. My shins were numb which meant it would be really hard to get up and run for the door. Plus there were probably multiple guards back there.

Lady Mairead leaned back in her seat, relaxed, comfortable. "I will tell ye a story of three men, daughter. I was born in Argyll. Has Magnus taken ye tae see his birthplace, the castle there?"

I shook my head.

"Tis beautiful, the loch, the castle, too bad ye haena seen it. I daena ken why our family prefers Balloch... Most of this time period is, as ye have seen, a bleak and brutal place, especially without a man tae protect ye. You learned this, I believe, when ye were taken away?"

"Yes."

"Must have been terrifying for ye, tae have nae knowledge Magnus was comin' for ye." She seemed to have lost her train of thought. Then she added, "I have had three protectors. They all had strengths and weaknesses. My first, Lowden, the father of Sean and Lizbeth, was a coarse barbarous fool. I believed him tae be strong and dashing, but he turned out tae be more impetuous and unreasonable. He died by the sword during a battle with Clan Donald, and I was relieved tae find another."

"Magnus's father?"

"Aye."

"I thought you told Magnus he was dead."

"He is nae alive in this time. He came tae me from the future."

"Oh."

"He is mighty. Powerful. Demanding. And once I was with child, he left tae go back tae his time."

I chewed my lip. "Why are you telling me this? You should tell this to Magnus."

"I am telling ye this because Magnus's father has given me a direct order, one I mean tae follow. And I winna let ye stand in my way."

"I don't understand."

"Magnus's father has promised me wealth and power in the future with him. His protection, as his wife, if I bring him a warrior, Magnus, when he is of age. You see? Magnus is an heir tae his father's throne and I will be there as the king's mother. If I can get him tae stay alive and ready tae fight for it."

I raised my head and leveled my gaze. "He won't fight for you, he won't do anything for you, not anymore."

"True, but he will fight for you. Though I haena finished my story." She watched me, her piercing gaze forcing my eyes down. "With Magnus's father's command, I sent Magnus tae London tae live at court, to be educated and gain the civilized manners he would need tae be a royal. When he turned eighteen he was brought tae Balloch so he could be trained in battle. He has been verra skilled at both. I, on the other hand, had tae protect myself. I married Delapointe. I gained a castle, riches, an army, yet, as ye know, my husband is a vindictive, evil man." She slowed to watch me again, her gaze causing me more discomfort than my knees.

"You have done me a service with your apt blow with a candlestick the other day. My dear Delapointe is quite senseless and bedridden. Perfectly so I would say. His death would have given me many complications, but his living on as a bedridden invalid — tis exactly the type of husband I need. I am unfettered but also un-widowed. Delapointe's son is furious. But tis tae be expected."

"So you owe me is what you're saying?"

"I'm saying, I am nae wantin' tae see ye die. And Magnus's father has taken a fancy tae ye—"

"Why, how?"

"I have been telling him of your escapades. He was verra proud of the way Magnus rescued ye from the men. Your movements through time are being tracked, and he has an interest in your actions. He has given me something ye may want as a peace offering." She watched me for a second. "Are you amenable tae making a deal?"

"Depends on what it is."

The side of her lip curled up. "Even with your husband tellin' ye nae? You would hear me on it?"

"Yeah, um, I guess so."

Her brow raised. "I am impressed with the amount of power

ye wield in your marriage, Kaitlyn Campbell. I dinna think ye would be capable of it, but ye have a strength I admire."

"Great." I said with as much ice as I could manage considering I was really greatly overpowered.

"Magnus's father has been verra pleased tae see Magnus figure out the math for the locations but there is one point Magnus haena been able tae understand."

"He can't figure out how to get to a specific time, the numbers don't make sense."

"Tis because we have kept an important piece from your vessels. Magnus's father has been choosing where Magnus would go and when he would arrive, giving him the challenge of it."

"Like a game? His father has been watching Magnus coming and going and deciding — oh my god..."

Lady Mairead held the small silver ring between her thumb and forefinger. "Magnus's father has given me permission to install this in your vessel. You will be able tae go home to whatever day ye wish. You will be able tae travel anywhere for as long as ye want and return without losing any time. I think ye would like this? You would get tae see your grandmother. Twould be a good thing for ye, I think?"

I nodded. "What would you want in return?"

"When Magnus is expected in his father's court, in six months time, he will be ready and able tae perform his duties."

"So Magnus would get to go home with me?"

"For about six months. You would have a chance tae be together without the troubles of the past tae worry about. He would only need tae keep in warrior shape for his ascension."

"Magnus will never agree. You should discuss this with him."

"He will agree, because ye will be wearing this." She held up the bracelet-sized ring.

"What is that?"

"It's a device which guarantees he will comply."

"What would it do to me?"

"Nothing, nae harm tae ye, as long as he comes when he is called." She shrugged. "If he daena come, then aye, it will cause ye harm."

"I'm not going to — you're crazy if you think..." My voice trailed off. "What if I say no?"

She scoffed. "Tis an excellent question dear daughter. Perhaps ye should consider what happens if ye daena agree."

"I guess you aren't just going to let me go?"

"What is my ultimate goal?"

"To have Magnus do your bidding in six months."

"If ye die today he will be upset. He may mourn ye long, but imprisoned he would have nae options but tae submit tae me. It might well be easier in the long run, but as I said, I am nae wanting tae see ye finished. I simply need ye tae be more controlled."

"You see that this is an impossible decision for me to make?"

"Nae. Tis an easy decision. You just have tae make it."

"If I take the deal, we can go back home to the day after we left?"

"And you can come back here and visit. You can come and go as ye please until Magnus is called for."

"My knees really hurt."

"Then you should make the decision quicker than this."

"If I say yes, you won't harass us, threaten my family, or bother us in any way?"

"I winna have a reason tae speak tae ye."

"And if I say no..."

"You winna see morning."

I gulped. "Can I speak to Magnus first?"

"Nae."

I nodded. I knew that would be her answer, but I was hoping to ask everything I could think of before agreeing. I knew I had to agree though, I didn't want to die, and I couldn't think of anything else to do. "Can you tell me what the ring does, how it works?"

"Nae. I daena know myself. I would imagine tis quite lethal. Possibly immediately so, but if the pain of the time vessel is any indication this may well be more painful. The inventors of these machines daena seem tae give a thought to mercy."

I sat back on my heels and nodded.

She raised her brow, waiting.

"Okay."

"You are saying aye tae my deal?"

I nodded again.

"I need ye tae say it louder."

"Yes."

She kept her gaze on my face.

I tried to meet her eyes. "Magnus will be ready for when he is called."

"Good. Verra good." She stood and crossed the floor to where I kneeled. The ring in her hand. She stood in front of me. "Raise your hair."

"Wait, what? I thought it was a bracelet." I raised my hair and flinched as she stretched the golden metal — it pulled open like putty — she brought it down over my head to my shoulders and released it. It felt like cold fingers as the ring grabbed around my throat, forming, tightening, panic-inducing.

"I don't think I can—" I tugged at it but it felt adhered to my skin. "I can't breathe."

"Aye, ye can breathe."

I gasped for air and tried to calm myself down. Clutching at the metal I heaved in a ragged breath. "I don't want to I—"

"Just breathe."

I dragged in a deep, stuttering breath.

"See? In a moment ye will nae remember tis there."

Tears welled up in my eyes.

She offered me a hand to help me stand.

I groaned and shook out my legs. My right one had gone to sleep. I banged it up and down and rubbed the kneecap while she retrieved one of the time vessels from a nearby table and fiddled with it for a moment and then unceremoniously passed it to me. The silver ring had been wrapped around the vessel.

"In the fourth series of numbers, now, ye simply add the date."

"Oh. Okay. What about the order, month and day and year, or the day the month the year?"

"The day, the month, the year." She said, "Kaitlyn, I will show ye tae your husband's room so ye may go."

I tried again, fruitlessly to get the ring around my neck to pry away. It felt snug, not in a good way, and while it had been about a half inch wide before, it was now foil-thin and about two inches wide. I took a step and stumbled on my half-dead left leg. It shot through with pins and needles.

"Follow me," Lady Mairead said.

CHAPTER 36

$\mathcal{I}$ rushed into the small prison room and sobbing into Magnus's arms. Lady Mairead stood at the door, flanked by two formidable guards. Magnus held me and spoke into my hair, "'Tis okay, Kaitlyn, okay."

"I had to, I had to do it." My face was pressed into his chest, sniveling into his skin.

He pulled my face up to his.

I cried harder looking at him. His face was broken. His skin marred, bruised, and split.

"What's this then?" He meant my words, but his one sort of opened eye saw my neck ring. He lifted my chin to inspect it, tried to peel it off. "Kaitlyn what is this?"

I sobbed harder. "I'm just going to wear it while—"

"Lady Mairead, what have ye done?"

"Your wife, Magnus, has been sensible enough tae make a deal with me. I have given her life. She has promised me yours. In six months time, ye will be my warrior and attend me tae ye father's court. If nae, she will take the punishment."

"I will go with ye, take it off her neck, I promise I will—"

"Tis too late tae be willing tae deal, your wife has stepped in where ye were incapable."

His arm went around me holding me to his chest.

"She has received a peace offering from me as well, a gift for ye both." She turned to go. "I will see ye in six months, Magnus."

"What about Kaitlyn, what will happen to her in six months?"

"I won't need her anymore." She departed through the door with the guards behind her. The door clanked shut as Magnus lunged for it.

He yelled though the door and struggled to open it. "What will you do to Kaitlyn in six months? Mairead, what is going to happen to Kaitlyn?"

There was no answer. Magnus stood, his hands on the door, his breaths coming in heaves.

What would happen to me when Lady Mairead didn't need me anymore? It was the big question and one I forgot to ask. But what would it have helped? Either I died today or six months from now, either way I was going to die.

I sank onto the cold stone floor. The sound of my collapse brought Magnus around. He strode to where I laid crumbled in a heap. "Kaitlyn?"

"Yeah?"

He lowered himself beside me. "You have the vessel?" He pulled me up into his lap, cradled in his arms.

"Yes, and she gave me a new part. If we say a date now, we can go to that date."

"Do ye remember the date we left?"

I nodded and curled into his arms, snuggling into this shoulder. "It's the fourth set of numbers." I gave him the date to use, one week after we left, so that it would make sense to our brains, our memories.

He pressed his cheek to my forehead and twisted the vessel, setting it pulsing to life. He began to recite the numbers while I held on around his neck, crying, going home.

CHAPTER 37

We must have landed in a sand dune. It was hot as hell. I had been sleeping, or whatever you called this thing after time-jumping where you lay unconscious just about dying of pain, for what felt like hours. Writhing. Screaming, sometimes internally, other times externally. Moaning too. I shook sand from my hair and checked Magnus. He shifted, thank god. I checked for my pouch. It was still around my waist. I dug through it for my phone.

I called Quentin.

That sound, the phone ringing, Quentin answering? Was the freaking best sound in the world. "Hi, we're back."

A moment later when I knew they were coming, I collapsed back in the sand. Then I rolled over and put an arm across Magnus's chest. "They're coming."

"Och, aye," he said and we lay there in the heat of a hot, very hot Florida day.

～

Quentin's face swam into focus. "Kaitlyn? Magnus? Jesus Christ Magnus, what happened to your face? Dude, I told you I should come with you, looks like you got your ass handed to you. Wow. Do you need a hospital?" He held out a hand for me and helped me to standing.

Magnus lumbered to his feet with a groan. He looked at Quentin through his swollen, black, lidded eyes, and chuckled. "What? This daena look like I won the fight?"

"Sir, it looks like you beat a man with your face. You have a sword, you shouldn't fight with your nose."

Magnus put out an arm, waving it in the air, helplessly. Quentin threw his shoulder under his arm and helped lift him to the car. "I have lost my sword."

"I see, along with your shirt and a good deal of your former good looks. How about you Katie, you okay?"

I limped behind them. "Besides being people-trafficked, having my life threatened, and PMSing in a cottage with a bunch of medieval madmen, yeah, I'm fine."

Quentin chuckled. "Man, that sounds fun. Boss, take me with you next time?"

I climbed in the back and Quentin helped Magnus lower into the passenger seat of the mustang, then asked me, "Want to drive?"

"I am in no condition to do anything but cry in a heap on the ground."

"Thought I'd ask." He jogged to the driver's seat.

"How long have we been gone?"

"One week." He roared the car to life. "We didn't have time to miss you."

"Thank god." At least Lady Mairead had been telling the truth about the vessel. My hand went to my throat. I felt along the edge of the ring. I could barely feel where my skin ended and the metal began. It was really terrifying, actually, how seamless my future death had become.

CHAPTER 38

ach and Emma, with the baby in her arms, met us in the garage at the bottom of the steps. When Magnus stepped from the car, Emma said, "Oh! Oh no, I'm going for the first aid kit..." She jogged up the steps.

We all followed Zach to the house. He walked backwards ducking his head under the ceiling as he climbed to the first floor, "Magnus, sir, what the fuck happened to your face?"

Quentin climbing the steps behind me said, "I told him if your face looks like that you aren't sword fighting right."

Magnus chuckled, his hand gripped the rail tightly, a slight limp to his climb. "'Tis verra funny."

Quentin's hand went protectively to my elbow helping to lift me because I was faltering, exhausted, pained, and apprehensive.

Magnus was made to sit at one of the kitchen stools where Emma assembled her supplies. Baby Ben was in the high chair beside her. She rifled through the box for bandages, ointments, anything, then said, "I don't know where to begin, you need a shower. Then I can bandage you."

Zach said, "What about steaks for those eyes?" He turned

from the fridge tearing open a butcher paper roll and pulling out two steaks. He held them out for Magnus.

"What are these for?"

"You put them on your eyes."

Magnus looked skeptical.

"Don't be a baby — sir, I mean, here, hold back your head." Chef Zach gingerly placed the steaks on Magnus's face, "Hold these in place."

"For what purpose?"

"The swelling. I don't know, I heard it works. Maybe it fucking doesn't at all, but at least your face is hidden for a while so I don't have a panic attack looking at you. What happened?"

"Lady Mairead's guards were teachin' me a lesson."

"Holy shit, that is one messed up mom you have."

"Chef Zach, I am terribly starved, am I tae eat these steaks after I wear them?"

Zach spun around and began searching the refrigerator shelves and the freezer, making his lists. "I have ice cream!"

Magnus's voice a bit muffled under the steaks. "Vanilla? Are there sauces for the top?"

"Caramel, fudge, marshmallow—"

"I will take them all."

Zach deposited a bunch of jars and cartons on the counter. "How about you, Katie, want ice cream?"

I gulped. My throat felt tight, not a lot, but a little, barely, but enough. My voice was so quiet that it shocked me. "Yes please."

Zach cocked his head to the side. "You're being really quiet, and what's with the new metallic neck tattoo?"

I burst into tears.

Magnus allowed the steaks to fall to the counter with a slurp sound and grabbed my hands. I cried, my shoulders shaking, huddled over my lap in my kitchen stool. This was not how my homecoming was supposed to be. How was I going to survive this fear?

Zach and Emma stood stock still. Baby Ben sat in his high chair banging his palms on the food tray, oblivious.

Quentin asked, "What happened to Katie?"

Magnus's head hung forward. His muscular hands enveloped mine. Strong, but not strong enough, not to protect me, not to rescue me. He had been in prison while I decided our fate, and I didn't know if I had made the right decision. And in a negotiation I ended up with a neck shackle. I clearly didn't negotiate well enough.

I smoothed my hair and wiped my cheeks. Emma rushed forward with a Kleenex, and I blew my nose. The snot of Scotland, three hundred years ago. When astronauts went to outer space, they had to clean thoroughly so they didn't introduce bizarre germs in a pristine environment. God, I needed a shower too.

I mumbled something to the effect of, "It's just a thing I have to wear and — I really need a shower."

Magnus's eyes met mine and he stood with a groan. "Aye, a shower, then we shall fill you all in on our adventures."

We left the room hand in hand while our family stood staring at our hunched, traumatized backs. Chef Zach said, "I'll keep the ice cream in the freezer for you."

"Aye, it might take centuries tae get this much grime from our skin."

A few moments later Magnus went to our bedroom door to call for help. "Emma, I could use some help here?"

She rushed in the room.

"I am trying tae work Kaitlyn's laces, but my hands are verra sore and nae workin' well."

She began tugging through the middle of the lacings, loosening, finally she said, "There ya go."

"Thank you." Tears welled up again.

"Want to step out of all your long underwear so I can take it to the laundry?"

"No. I didn't—" I took a deep breath to try to fight back the tears that wanted to come. "I ruined the underwear. I left it there. I didn't have my stuff."

"Aw, Katie, that sucks. Hey, Zach was thinking you guys might want some McDonalds tonight — he's running out to pick it up?"

I really did start crying. "Really? That would be amazing. Thank you."

She called into the bathroom. "Magnus, is McDonalds okay with you for dinner?"

He called back. "If there's ice cream, and Kaitlyn wants it."

"Yeah." I said, "I'll take a shower. Once I eat I'll stop being such a crybaby, and we can maybe burn everything in a bonfire."

"Good. Perfect. Let me know if you need anything."

"Just Hayley."

"I'll call her and tell her it's an emergency." She left and I stepped from my clothes leaving a big pile I kicked so any stains would be hidden. And met my husband in the bathroom.

He had started the shower. The temperature was perfect. He held my hand, led me into the water, worried over my step, let me go under the shower first and treated me like an invalid. I let the shower round down my head, my face, mixing with my tears to cover me, a waterfall of water, fresh and salty, the sound of water falling to drown out everything else.

Magnus stood beside me, wet flesh, muscle-bound, solid. Where I stood, he pressed into my space, just by standing there.

After my turn under the water, I stepped to the side, and he took his turn, ducking under the water, with a, "Phwesha!" Flicking his hair, beginning to press his palms to his face, but stopping in time and instead, rubbing the width of his shoulders.

He looked at me finally. One eye barely visible in the swollen mass of purple. His lopsided cracked smile was sad. One of those sad, sad smiles. Almost more sad than no smile at all.

I looked down at the ground, squirted shampoo in my hand and began lathering my hair, eyes closed. No sad smiles, please. No. I didn't need placating looks, or invalid helps — I needed answers. Like how was I going to live with this thing around my neck? What was going to happen to me in six months? What was going to happen to Magnus when he was called on? Would we be okay? Were we okay now?

Soon we were in pajamas.

Back on the stools with bags of McDonalds all over the counter. Our burgers placed decoratively on nice plates. Beers in front of us. The sweet decadent sheer swollen size of the food, and the endless beers, each coming before I even needed the next one, began to work on my mood.

When Hayley appeared, alone, so she could hear about our adventures, I even laughed when Magnus joked, "I know, I shouldna have beat that man with my face, but he deserv'd it."

And then Hayley, eyes leveled on me, said, "Out with it, the whole story, ending with that metallic neck-thing you have there."

"So I was people trafficked while I was PMSing."

"Jesus Christ girlfriend, what kind of god-forsaken vacation did you go on?"

"As you know, it wasn't a vacation, we were going to rescue Magnus's brother from Lord Delapointe, who, by the way, is still an invalid from the knock upside the head I gave him."

"Nicely done."

My eyes met Magnus's. He was looking at me through that slit in his swollen eyes, head cocked back to see better. The look was appreciative. Like he thought I was great. And yes, I was beginning to feel a tiny bit better.

Zach slid another beer in front of me.

"We rescued Sean. It was awesome."

Quentin asked, "How'd you do it?"

"I blinded them with those flashlights like we discussed. Worked great. But then we waited in the woods with a bunch of men for the guards to come out and fight."

Quentin leaned forward. "How many men?"

Magnus said, "I had about twenty-three. Some mercenaries I dinna trust, but some of my cousins."

I said, "At dawn the guards from the castle came to the field and Magnus and our men were fighting them, and it was this huge melee."

Quentin said, "Like Warcraft or something?"

"Totally."

"Man I would have liked to see that."

"Lizbeth's husband was dying though." I took another swig of beer. "I dragged him to the trees—"

Hayley started waving her hands, "Whoa whoa whoa, dying? Like literally *dying?*"

Magnus said, "Och, aye."

"Dying?"

"It was a battle, Hayley. Men were fighting with swords everywhere and guns, really old guns, were going off. Yes, people were going to die. One of them happened to be Magnus's brother-in-law. I was pressing on his wound trying to stop the flow of blood when suddenly I was grabbed from behind, thrown on a horse, and stolen away." I peeled the label from my beer.

Chef Zach said, "What the fuck?"

I pointed at him. "Exactly. This is what is going through my mind. I'm upside down over the back of a horse, hurts like hell, there are like five men, all these horses, and there are no phones, no police, no nothing. I decided to pass out. I woke up hours later, really far away, and those assholes just laughed at me."

Hayley snapped her fingers and pointed at her beer. "Refill please, Zach. What the heck did you do?"

"Nothing. I thought through it all and there was nothing to do. It was freezing. I didn't know the language. Had no idea where I was. They said Magnus was dead. I just gave up. And — drumroll please, that's when my period started."

Emma had her hands over her mouth. "Was it bad?"

"Yep."

Quentin asked Magnus, "How did you find her?"

"I tracked the men, inquired at villages they passed. I was about a day behind, but they dinna ken I was following them. I made up time and got tae them on the third day."

"Three days?" Hayley and Emma said in unison.

I nodded solemnly. "I have never been so happy than when Magnus barreled down the hill with his sword drawn, slashing those assholes left and right. He was so freaking awesome."

"Five men — you fought them alone?" asked Quentin.

Magnus shrugged. "I only managed tae kill one. They werena in it for anythin' but the payment. They ran when they saw I planned tae make it difficult for them tae keep livin'."

Hayley said, "This is just like a movie. What the hell? I can't believe this is real life."

"I know." I said. "He fought them while I lay on the edge of the battlefield with my uterus twisting around my ovaries."

Emma and Hayley both screwed their faces up in commiseration.

"Then we went back to Balloch Castle for the funerals, and we thought that was all we needed to do. Then we would time-jump home. But somehow Lady Mairead circumvented us and brought us to Talsworth. Do you know how she did it?" I asked Magnus.

"Nae, I woke up in the prison."

"Me too." I reached for his hand and clutched it in my lap. "She told me this whole long story about her life, and I was thinking, 'You are so freaking evil you're even doing that villainous gloating thing.'" I took another big swig of beer. "She told me that Magnus's father is alive and wants him, in six months, to come to the future and take the throne or something. Lady Mairead thinks it will be her big moment when she and Magnus go there."

I glanced at Magnus his brow was furrowed. "Did she say it like that, 'take the throne?'"

I thought for a moment. "I don't really remember how she said it. It's hazy. I was kind of freaking out. Her guards were beating you in front of me. It was hard to think. My impression was she needed you to be ready to fight."

Magnus looked down at his beer bottle and gave it a spin.

Chef Zach said, "Need another, boss?"

"What? Och, aye." Another beer was placed in front of him. He asked me, "She didn't say anything else about what would happen in six months?"

"No, just for you to be ready. That she would call." I looked around the room. "Also that she wouldn't cause any trouble. We're all safe now."

Hayley asked, "Good. That's good. Magnus will just go be a warrior-prince six months from now. He'll handle that, like a business trip, and it will all be fine. Right?"

Magnus said, "Aye, I'll handle it."

Hayley giggled, "See, when you hear him say it like that," her voice went low. "'Aye, I'll handle it,' you know he's going to do it. So what about the golden neck wrap?"

"This is an enticement for Magnus to come when they call."

Hayley squinted her eyes. "Enticement?"

I ran my fingers up and down on the foil, it felt cold to my fingertips, and I could feel my fingertips through it. "Yeah. If he doesn't show up when they call, something happens to me."

"What the fuck kind of sick—"

"I know. We don't know what it is, what it does. But I've been told that it's lethal. It changed shape to mold to my neck. My guess is it cuts off my air supply, because it kind of feels like it already."

Everyone sat quietly. It was clear on their faces that they didn't know what to say.

Magnus put a big solid hand on my shoulder and gave it a squeeze, then he ran it down my arm and pulled me across the space to his chest and hugged me for a moment. Once released I sat back up.

"The other thing I got from Lady Mairead was a small piece to fit on our time travel vessel that brought us to whatever date we wanted. We chose today and here we are." I tried to smile.

Hayley looked at Magnus. "So you have six months to get that thing off her neck."

"Aye."

I said, "But also, we have six months, no Lady Mairead, no nothing to do, nobody to rescue. I can finally start on that list of places I want to take Magnus. So don't be so glum." I finished a beer and slammed it to the table. "Don't be glum."

CHAPTER 39

*W*ith my toothbrush in my mouth and toothpaste spit rolling down my chin I said, "Thank you for letting me tell the battle tales tonight. I feel better."

"You needed tae tell them, twas in your eyes."

I spit and wiped my mouth. "Is that how it works?"

"After a battle ye have tae drink and tell the stories and all your friends have tae listen, even if they were at the battle too. Because ye canna keep it inside, it has tae be told." He wiped his mouth too.

"Well, it's not like I was actually battling. I didn't really do anything. I mean, if you think about it, I just mostly screwed up and you had to rescue me over and over."

"Tis how ye see it?"

"You don't see it like that?"

"Nae, ye did it right. Ye dinna run and hide in the woods. I would have never found ye, ye know." He pulled close and tucked my hair behind my ear. "Ye dinna cause them tae leave ya, and most important of all, ye dinna get killed."

I looked at him for a moment. "Well, when you put it that way, I guess I was kind of awesome."

"And I screwed up too, as ye say. I refused tae discuss the matter with Lady Mairead, I left ye tae do it." He leaned against the bathroom counter. He fiddled with my brand new Burt's Bees lip balm. "Twas nae fair tae leave ye there."

"My recollection is that you had at least four armed men that wouldn't let you stay."

"Still. Tis a regret of mine."

I returned to our bedroom, undressed, and climbed into the covers. Magnus came a moment later, turned out lights as he undressed, and climbed in after me. It was a hot night, but I hadn't been out in it at all, and our house was cool. The AC was running full blast. I pulled the comforter over me, a luxury I desperately needed. To think of it — fast food, beer, friends, air conditioning, and a comforter — when only a few days ago I believed I was dead. I needed it all.

Magnus snuggled in on his side and scooped me up by the hips and pulled me to him. My upper thigh wrapped across his waist. His forearm around my ass. My upper arms around his head. His injured face nuzzled into my breasts.

He kissed me and ran his tongue along my skin, his hand trailing down my back, bringing me closer. I kissed his forehead — that taste of salt on my tongue. His smell filled my lungs and warmed me as his fingers felt their way between the soft folds between my legs and entered me. He played there, tantalizing and slow, as if he had all the patience in the world while my excitement grew dripping and wanting, and — *come here* — I was breathless, impatient and ready. I tugged at his back trying to urge him upward.

He paused.

The only sounds were my breaths and the only movements my wiggles against his solid, immobile body. "Magnus?" His face nuzzled into my skin. I pulled away and attempted to lift his chin. "What's happening?"

"I canna..."

"Can't what?"

"Canna look on it."

"On me?" The words squeaked out. "Me?" I wanted to beat him, pummel him with blows, but I also wanted to curl up in a ball and cry again and I had been trying to be a better person. All of these thoughts were a cruel joke — his skin was too marred to beat.

"When I see it I am ashamed at what I let happen tae ye." His voice came from low, below my breast..

I flipped onto my back. "These are the words of failure Magnus Campbell. The kind of words that shouldn't be spoken into the springs of our marital mattress. I'm going to have to smudge this whole room tomorrow."

"What do ye mean, smudge?"

"It's like witchcraft but without the actual witchcraft and doesn't matter at all when I'm confronted with a husband that doesn't want to look at me, can't look at me anymore. You know your face isn't looking that great either."

He sighed. "You know that inna what I mean."

I wanted to kick and scream and tear at my gold-plated neck, while he needed kisses and loving guidance. How to reconcile the two things? I couldn't possibly be the person to give him guidance about this. About me. Not now. But I had to. Had to.

I curled back on my side, my lips pressed to his head. "I love you," I said. "Let's just lay here and breathe together for a moment." I wrapped my arms around and held him in a tight hug to my chest. I took a deep calming breath and another, letting my chest rise and fall against his cheek. My heart beat sure and strong. His warm breath on my breast. "I love you." I said again.

"I know ye do, mo reul-iuil, because ye carry a cartload of my horse shit without complaint."

I chuckled with my lips close to his skin. "Oh I complain, I just keep it inside. It pours out later as snarky jokes."

His hand trailed down my back again. He was becoming comfortable. His breaths joining mine.

"You know, I haven't really seen it either. It is hard to look at."

His cheek stubble shifted on the soft skin of my breast.

I tilted back my head exposing my throat and waited for him to decide he could. Finally his head lifted and his fingers trailed along the pulse at the side of my neck. I said, "I can feel your fingers through it."

"I can feel your beat." His fingers felt along the edge, then he pushed me to my back and rested on his elbows on each side of my head, his solid body pressing down on mine in all the best comfortable, necessary ways. When I looked up at his face, black and blue and swollen, I had to close my eyes, but it was okay if he was on me, would be better when he was in me.

He pushed hair from my cheek and then ducked down to kiss me on the gold plating around my throat. "It gives ye a different taste."

I arched my neck, more, more. He sucked and kissed on my pulse bringing pleasure to the spot that threatened pain someday and it felt so good. I pulled his buttocks, firm and hard, oh so much closer. My breaths had gone shallow and fast again — *you want me?*

— *och aye* —

You can look on me? I ran my hand down his back, pulling and pushing against his solid mass. My legs parted wide and he slid inside me. His breath a moan against my neck.

He didn't answer — lost in my body — I asked him again — *can you see me?*

—*Aye, I see you*—

I stretched my arms over my head. "What do you see?"

He rose above me, pushing into me — *my Kaitlyn* — He pushed against me harder, deeper with force and power — *my home.*

I wrapped my legs around him meeting his power with my own.

CHAPTER 40

*T*he next couple of weeks we made a plan. We knew we didn't have much time like this and Magnus needed to prepare for whatever was in store. What would that preparation be? We were talking about it slowly. Quentin was coming up with a schedule. We were going to bulk him up, build his muscles, spar more, hire a trainer. The plan was unfolding, but in the meantime I wanted to show him a little of the modern world

I went through my list and crossed off everything that would require plane flight because getting through TSA would be impossible. That narrowed it down to driving. I decided that heading south to Orlando would be fun for a long weekend.

And we would drive by Kennedy Space Center too.

As we made our plans, we smiled more. I reserved a hotel and picked the restaurants and had a literal binder with printed pages of ideas. We laughed and teased and generally got past the fear and torment of our past experiences. I marveled at our resilience actually — we could go through so much and still love each other.

We had so much to be afraid of yet we were happy.

Some days I did feel as if it was a kind of magic in our bond. What had he said, 'Tis as if we were meant tae be'?

I liked that, it made me feel special.

And I mostly never thought about the cruel plating around my neck.

CHAPTER 41

*T*wo days before our trip we went for a morning run on the beach, Magnus, Quentin, and I. It was a good one, the day was beautiful, cool. The sun was bright overhead and it shimmered on the pools of water left by the low tide. We had splashed through some shallow ones while we ran, barefoot.

When we were done Magnus and Quentin headed back for the house, but I decided to linger for a moment. The tide was low, the shells were abundant. I found two beautiful shells that I wanted to keep, broken conchs, but their internal twists were exposed, colorful, smooth, and shiny. I found three small sharks teeth and dropped them into the cell phone pocket of my yoga pants.

I decided to head to the house for some water.

Quentin was stationed up on the roof deck. He lifted his hand in a wave as I climbed to the boardwalk. He was always watching. I was becoming used to it I supposed, but still. My view of the house always included a guard stationed on one of the decks. Like a weathervane, checking the sky for the storms.

We didn't really think we needed the constant surveillance

anymore, Lady Mairead promised we would have peace for six months, but she was not to be trusted so here we still were.

Magnus was sitting in one of our chairs in front of the sliding doors. Elbows on his knees, intently watching me walk up the boardwalk. His gaze constant.

And as I drew closer, his smile widened.

He shook his head slowly that kind of movement that means what I'm seeing is so profoundly awesome I am shaking my head in disbelief. And that was pretty fabulous. To be loved by him this much.

I grinned back.

And as I drew closer I noticed he was raising his brow, grinning, and his expression had turned into — what would it be called? — cocksure. Pleased with himself. And he was chuckling too.

"What?"

"Why dinna ye tell me?"

I squinted my eyes. "Tell you what?"

His expression didn't falter, and his eyes literally twinkled. Like he had a joke and he was trying to keep it from me while letting me know he had a joke.

I stood four feet in front of him and said, "Okay, out with it."

"I have conquered ye."

I scoffed. "First of all love isn't a battle. Yes, I love you desperately. Yes, I married you. Yes, I'm yours, but I'm not conquered."

His eyes twinkled and I swear to god his grin got even wider, more cocky. I play stamped my foot, "Plus I married you quite a while ago. And that cocky-ass grin is growing wider by the minute. Are you up to something? What did you do?"

His left brow lifted up and down. "Aye, I am tellin' ye, I conquered ye. And inna about the love. Though twas quite masterful at gettin' ye tae love me — I am verra proud of the fact. And tis nae on the marriage, twas by contract as ye ken. Though

I think I may have brought my irresistible charm tae the matter—"

"Irresistible?"

"Aye."

I rolled my eyes. "You are positively gloating. And it's hot out here." I put the shells on the deck railing and fanned myself. "Out with it or I'm going to tell you I don't care about it at all and brush by you into the house. And then you'll be sitting out here gloating to yourself."

"Okay, I will be quick on the matter. I have conquered ye, Kaitlyn Campbell, ye are with bairn."

"What the — what? Bairn — a baby? What? You think I'm pregnant?"

"Aye tis verra clear."

My hand reflexively went to my stomach. "Magnus are you calling me fat?"

"I am calling ye pregnant." His eyes twinkled even more.

"I am on the pill, I'll have you know."

"That wee pill ye take in the mornin'? Apparently twas nae match for my great manliness." He sprawled back in the chair and even gave a small gesture to his lap. "I have gotten ye with child." His grin, I hardly thought possible, even wider.

"Well, it's not true. I think I would know. It is my body after all. I don't know why you would think you'd know before me."

Magnus picked up a towel and scrubbed it up and down on his face. It was getting very hot out here, the cool morning switching to the high heat of the noonday sun. "I ken it because tis verra plain. Remember two nights ago when ye were randy and climbed on me in the night, astride, and galloped along at a quick, brazen pace?"

"Brazen? It's not how I remember it, but yes?"

"I cupped m'hands around your breasts. Ye like it when I do, and it helps tae keep your rhythm steady. Else ye grow wild." My eyes grew wide. Magnus ignored me and carried on, his expression proving he was enjoying the moment immensely. "You were jigglin' up and down on my palms and it came tae me that your breasts are heavier than afore. Sean said twas how he ken his wife was carryin' a bairn. Your breasts," he acted out cupping his hands, "usually the weight and size of a hen's egg are much more like an apple. Twas noticeable."

"My breasts are much bigger than an egg and I thought you weren't to take advice from your brother anymore." My arms folded across my chest, almost without thinking about it.

"Aye, twas why I dinna ken it right then, I had tae think on it longer. Yesterday I was thinkin' on it when we were in the shower together and ye were bent over and I was behind ye and—"

His grin was fully mischievous.

"I know what we were doing." I gestured for him to continue.

"When my palms were on your haunches, directing ye, it came tae me, twas wider than afore. Ye—"

"Magnus, you were measuring and weighing me while we were making love?"

He chuckled. "Your body tis as my own, mo reul-iuil. And your rump daena fit in my palm's width a'more. Twas extra. I was startled by it. Almost lost m'focus."

"So again, you're saying I'm fat. I'm not pregnant, I would know."

"My uncle Baldie told me twas a sign a horse is foalin' tae have its haunches widen. Tis a sign."

I sighed and feigned despair. "Now you are comparing me to a horse, good sir. You will need to be soooo romantic to make this whole conversation up to me."

He waved my words away. "And I was thinkin' on it more tryin' tae decide about it and just now as ye walked up the boards I could hear it in your step, heavy, your gait wide." He reached out for my foot. I pulled it away and he left his seat, diving for it and holding it firm. I giggled.

"See here?" He tickled my instep and I giggled more. "Has lowered, just a modicum, barely, but enough that your step has gone from a light prance to a bit of a lumber, not much mind ye —" I swatted his shoulder.

"Magnus, I am not pregnant."

He dropped my foot with a laugh. "Och aye, when ye have grown squat as a brooding hen we will see if I am right."

I had my hands on my hips looking down at him. "We can know right now. And if you are wrong, which you are, without a doubt, you will need to make this up to me. I think our love-making tonight will need to be all you doing whatever I want."

He grinned and shrugged. Looking up at me from near my feet. "Tis nae matter, whether tis a lost wager or a celebration, I will do what ye want, but if I am right ye will have tae call me Master Magnus through it." He chuckled.

I pushed him playfully. "Get in the car."

CHAPTER 42

*M*agnus was wearing his kilt, with a modern T-shirt, a pale sky blue, my favorite color, and a pair of Nikes. They were a neutral color, cool looking, expensive. He loved them, having worn wrapped leather around his feet most of his life. He grabbed one of those half-sized shopping carts which looked pretty ridiculous with his hulking mass pushing it and wandered off towards the middle of the store which was set up with seasonal 'summer' equipment.

I headed straight for the family planning section and stood in front of the pregnancy tests trying to decide between the best price on a three pack or paying extra for a single test. Why would I need more than one? Would I need more than one to prove to Magnus that I wasn't? Would I need more than one in case he did this every single month?

He wandered up, his cart full. "Magnus, you do not get out enough," I teased. On top of the pile was a battery-powered hand-held plastic fan with a water bottle connected to it, for misting. That would be useful actually at Disney world.

He asked, "Did you find what ye needed?"

Then his eyes fell on a box and he lifted it from the shelf and tossed it on top of the pile in his shopping cart basket.

"Do you even know what that is?"

"Nae, I like the picture of the helmet."

"It's a Trojan helmet and a box of, let me see—" I picked up the box, "Forty-eight condoms." I watched his brow draw down in with his confused look. "They're for wrapping around your cock during sex so there won't be a pregnancy."

He took it from my hand and grinned. "But see, we winna be needin' them, the deed is done." He returned it to their place on the shelf.

I rolled my eyes, for like the hundredth time that morning, and pulled the three-pack of pregnancy tests off the shelf and tossed it in the cart.

CHAPTER 43

*I*t only took twenty minutes to get home, deposit the shopping bags full of Magnus's loot in the kitchen, and now we were in our bathroom. I ripped the packaging open and pulled out a pregnancy test stick. Magnus watched quietly, captivated, checking the box and opening the massive instructions. I didn't need the instructions. This one was as easy as one, two, pee.

I stripped my yoga pants to my ankles and unceremoniously sat on the toilet. We hadn't been around each other for that long but we weren't private about our body functions. In the 1700s we had no bathrooms, in 2018 we had a frosted glass door. Plus we had both given instructions to the other. Teaching someone how to use the bathroom put a familiarity to it, I supposed.

Once my butt hit the toilet seat Magnus slid down the wall opposite me and, still holding the instructions, watched.

I couldn't pee.

"Can you get me some water?"

Magnus stood to get one of our cups from the counter, filled it with tap water and handed it to me. Then he dropped back to his place. "It says here ye need tae pee on it."

"I'm trying." I held the stick at the ready between my legs and screwed up my face funny.

He chuckled. "If we were a four-hour ride from the next chamberpot ye would need tae go."

"Yep, it's always at the most inopportune moments."

Finally, it came with a rush and the stick was doused in the stream, as per the instructions.

"What do I do next?" I shook the liquid off it.

Magnus read, "We wait three minutes for a sign."

I looked down at the stick, there was an unmistakable plus sign.

Without a doubt.

I stared at it dumbfounded.

"Kaitlyn?"

"I'm pregnant." I turned the stick around so he could see the mark.

He smiled sadly. "I told ye."

"You did, you won."

Sadder still he said, "Aye. I have won."

Clutching the pregnancy test stick in my fist I stood and wriggled my yoga pants up, dropped to the ground and climbed into my husband's arms. "I have this thing around my neck. What if I die? What if something happens to me and it involves a baby?"

"Aye, but I winna let anythin' happen tae ye, Kaitlyn. I daena believe Lady Mairead will keep ye in the neck shackle once she ken a bairn is comin'. She has wanted me tae be motivated tae fight for her as her warrior. I have motivation now, I want tae keep ye safe. I think she will discuss the matter with me and we can come to an understandin' on it."

"You think?"

"I am sure of it. Twould be her descendent. She will take it seriously."

"How would you talk to her about it?"

"I daena ken. I think I would have tae journey to see her."

"That sounds dangerous."

"Twould be, but necessary. And after we discuss it, the danger would be past."

"I won't be able to go with you. I'll be here, and you'll have to go without me and — what are we going to do?" I buried my face into his sky blue shirt.

"Aye, ye winna be able tae travel for a verra long time." We both sat very very quietly. Magnus pulled up my fist and turned it gently to see the plus sign. He was thoughtful on it for a few moments and then he allowed my hand to drop to the floor and his head went back against the wall with a sigh.

He started to speak then stopped then began again. "First, we are goin' tae give me a day tae crow around here like a conquering hero who has gotten his wife with bairn. Do you think Master Peters and Cook would come and listen tae me carry on about it? Would they think me heroic?"

I smiled. "They will probably think you're a little insane for being as excited as you are. Modern men generally see it as a great deal of responsibility, perhaps too much."

"Och aye, tis a great deal of responsibility. But if I provide them with ale and a bit of loud storytellin' they might rally tae the excitement of it."

"Probably." I took a deep breath.

"But then Kaitlyn, after that day tae crow, I will — I want ye tae ken I take this matter verra serious. I have been thinkin' it is a battle I must win, but I understand now tis life and death. Your life and death, and I winna let anythin' happen tae ye. I winna. You have my word. I will protect ye, I will protect our bairn." He pressed his lips to my hairline, just above my worried brow. "I winna be mistaken, I promise. You winna have tae live in fear."

"I know. And you'll train and when Lady Mairead calls on you to be her warrior—"

"I am nae her warrior. I fight only for you."

~

I closed my eyes. Snuggled on my husband's chest the world didn't feel any different. Whatever he said, I didn't feel changed at all but the world had changed so much. My feeling about it. I was still reeling from the fear about my neck piece, and now somehow I was going to need to rally to become the kind of person who could take care of someone else. I would have to become really really strong and from here, on my bathroom floor, curled up on Magnus's chest didn't feel like a good start. I felt weak as hell. I was going to be left alone again. Magnus would be taking care of all of this and I would be alone, here, being strong enough to take care of a baby.

How would that even work?

It was going to take every single ounce of strength I had. I would need to pull up my big girl panties and — my pregnancy panties. I gulped and like most of the time in moments of duress I went for sarcasm. "So I guess if you think about it, undying love and promising to protect me forever — I conquered you."

"Aye Kaitlyn, ye have." He kissed my forehead. "But for this day I will crow about the conquering I've done."

I pulled away and watched his face. "You are serious about this, huh? You are such a man."

He grinned.

I brushed the hair back from my face and settled across his lap, leaned on his knees, facing him. "Explain it to me so I can understand from your perspective."

His smile widened. "See, mo reul-iuil, tis as if ye are a castle. A beautiful castle and I want tae live there. I have been battering at the walls with my cannon—"

"You sir are incorrigible."

He continued, "I dinna want tae break the castle mind ye, because I want tae—"

"Live there, I know, I get the metaphor," I laughed.

"But ye had a guard stationed on the walls. I daena blame ye for it. Twas smart tae do it. I was actually quite glad of it that I could batter away with my—"

"Big cannon."

"Exactly! Have I told ye today that ye are a good wife?"

"No, if I recall you have called me fat, compared me to a horse, and are now waxing poetic about battering my walls."

"You are a verra good wife."

"Okay go on with your big cannon," I giggled, feeling much better actually.

"I was quite enjoying myself. And expectin' your guard tae meet me on the rampart, yet here we are, I have vanquished your guard, battered your walls, and now one of my warriors is living right there in that beautiful castle." He put a hand on my stomach. "Tis truly mine now."

I sighed. Happily. But I teased him, "It's one way of putting it, I suppose. Or you could say I screwed up earlier in the month. When we returned from Scotland, I had just had my period, but with the time jumping we hadn't missed a day, so I couldn't figure out when to start my next pack of pills, so I didn't for a couple of days until I realized that didn't make sense and started taking them. In the meantime, probably that night a few weeks ago where you were doing that thing and I was—"

"Twas exactly that night. You were spectacular, all moans and writhin'. I knew then I had won."

"Well, whatever the outcome, I liked it very much, you can do that anytime."

We sat for a moment and grinned at each other.

"So your sperm met my egg and worked together to create a baby inside my uterus. But for today I will agree that you have conquered my walls and stand victorious. With your warrior inside me drinking mead and eating turkey legs or whatever it is that your little warrior will do."

"That's the spirit, mo reul-iuil."

"I'm sure Michael and James and Quentin and everyone else will come over and—" My eyes went wide. "Oh no, I have to tell Hayley."

"She will be sharp on the matter I would expect, I daena think she likes the idea much."

"She doesn't. When she has a baby, she needs a nursery like Lizbeth has, upstairs, so she can deposit the baby and other people can take care of it." I sighed again. "I won't be able to see Lizbeth."

"Aye. Twill be a long time I expect."

"I miss her. And it's..." I was going to say, poignant, that the missing was so far in the past. I was speaking to Lizbeth just the other day, but she lived a long long time ago. She was part of a long hazy long ago past. And being there was the only thing that kept her living. I was going to say all of that but it would have involved Magnus as well. He was supposed to be living then, yet here he was, living now. And much like not knowing what day to take my pill, which year was the passage of time being counted on? The here and now? Or were days in the past counted too. And at what rate? I folded my head back to Magnus's chest. "We should get up from the bathroom floor, probably."

"And make our announcement."

CHAPTER 44

*Z*ach and Emma were thrilled. Most of the gang came over and Zach put out appetizers and drinks and we celebrated. Hayley was discombobulated by the news, most of the boys were skeptical that it was good news, but shortly after their arrival Magnus had everyone believing it was the best news ever, because he so believed it to be. We were having a baby. It was going to ground me from adventures, from journeying with him, but really, that might not be a bad thing. We were staying here for the next six months, anyway. And then Magnus would get called upon to do his thing.

His mysterious thing.

Some kind of warrior thing.

And I would stay here.

And somehow the gold band around my neck would end up being nothing, an idle threat.

The night had been good and I was beginning to feel the warm glow coming up, like a beam from my center. I was going to have Magnus's child. When I caught his eye from across the room his smile and gaze was so smoldering hot and meant for just me that it made me blush.

Yes.

Aye.

Emma answered a million questions for me. And she called in a favor with a friend who was a receptionist and got me an appointment for the next day with a local OB/GYN.

We were full of long quiet nervous pauses as I drove us to the OB's office. I was wearing one of my most grownup outfits, a sundress that went to my knees and a pair of sandals with closed toes. Magnus seemed really nervous. He was wearing one of his modern kilts, and kept adjusting his shirt as if it was constricting his lungs. I was taking deep breaths trying to draw air past my constricted throat. "Ready?"

"Ready."

On the way he asked, "What are they goin' tae do tae ye, Kaitlyn?"

"I don't a hundred percent know? I think I have to pee in a cup. Emma mentioned that. She said maybe I'd have a sonogram? I don't really know at all. I just nodded and smiled. While she was pregnant, there were a lot of books around the house, but I didn't read them. I didn't think it would apply to me."

His brow was drawn down but he didn't seem to have anymore questions and I was too nervous to think of things to tell him.

I parked the car.

We walked to the hospital building and as I reached for the front door I felt him slow and stop. He took a step back.

"What's happening?" I let the door close.

"I daena want tae go in. I haena good memories of these places."

He looked up at the building facade and around the front step. Another couple approached, the woman had a very rounded pregnant belly, and we stepped out of the way so they could enter.

He continued, "I daena understand what they are sayin' in hospitals, and tis all verra confusing. I daena ken how tae protect ye here."

"Yeah..." I gave him a sad smile. "But I think all men have that problem on a day like today. In a place like this. And women, if it's their first time. We're going into a big unknown. But we're doing it together. Me, you, and the warrior you put in my castle."

He smiled a little. "'Twas yesterday. Today I have made my Kaitlyn with bairn and I daena — tis verra dangerous."

"Well, that being true, it's not as dangerous anymore. You've seen me do a lot of things and women all over the world do this, I can, for sure. This shit is handled. See my belly?" I pulled my dress over my flat stomach. "I can do this."

"What if he can tell that I am from the past? What if it — what if the baby is—" He shook his head.

"Are you worried something's wrong with the baby?"

He nodded. Looking down at the ground.

"Because you're from the past?"

His nod was barely perceptible, but he looked me in the eyes. "What if there is a price I have tae pay?"

"Magnus, there is no price. There is just me and you. We love each other, we made a baby, and we're going to do everything we can do to make it a happy healthy baby. We're no different from any other couple. They won't know you're from the past. We won't tell them. We're going to go upstairs. You're going to nod and smile and look handsome. And listen. I will ask questions. They will poke and prod me and we will both accept that as expected and then we'll go home and have a dinner to celebrate. And tell our staff we thought it was easy. Easy. Okay?"

Magnus nodded. "Okay, mo reul-iuil. I'm following you."

We went up the stairs to the office.

And emerged an hour and ten minutes later.

We turned the car on, air conditioning full-blast, and sat there. Breathing. Occasionally looking at the photo Magnus held in his hand. It was from the sonogram. A photo of the clump of cells that made up our baby. Our baby.

Magnus stared at it long.

"Tis a miracle."

I wasn't sure if he was thinking about the technology that made it possible for us to have a video of a beating heart, a still photo of our baby, or that he got me pregnant past my pill, or that me and him, Kaitlyn from now, Magnus from the long ago past had somehow combined our genetic history and would be passing it down through our descendants. He was thinking about all of that maybe. And me too. It was a miracle through and through.

"You ready to go home?"

"Och aye." He said, so I drove us home.

CHAPTER 45

$\mathcal{T}$he next morning with a lot of fanfare and fuss we said goodbye to our staff and house and loaded ourselves up into an RV. It was called a Thor Chateau, and the name was half the reason I rented it. The other half was that it had seven foot high ceilings.

I pulled from the driveway, our staff waving goodbye from the garage, and said, "Well, let's see if I can drive this."

Magnus chuckled and closed his eyes.

My plan was to take us to Orlando. We had a camping spot at Disney World reserved and we were going to spend tomorrow at the park. I knew it was going to be insanely crowded, very hot, and mostly impractical, but it had been on my list of things to show him. So I was making it happen. I wouldn't put it off. Couldn't.

After Disney World we were headed south to a camping spot outside of Miami. I thought we would go out to dinner, somewhere fun and possibly glamorous, and so we had our nice clothes hanging in the RV's closet. And then we would drive all the way down to Key West. I had never done that part of the trip and we only got a camping spot because of sheer luck and a lot of cash. But that was fine. Zach offered to fly down, whenever and wherever we needed, to make us dinner. Which was really sweet but totally unnecessary.

Quentin offered to drive but we left him at the house as a guard. We talked it over the night after we visited the OB and decided to take the time-travel vessel to the bank and put it in a deposit box. It was tracking us, we had no doubt. Lady Mairead wasn't going to follow us, but we decided to be safe.

At first, as we drove, I excitedly pointed at things out the window. "Have you ever seen one of those trucks?" Or "Okay this is a treat, check out this bridge." Magnus would force his eyes open and try to seem interested, then would clamp his eyes shut again.

Finally I listened to the radio, loud, singing along to Ed Sheeran. I glanced over at him. "You cool?"

"We are goin' verra fast."

"True, compared to the average speed on the Island which is 20 miles per hour, yes..." I looked at the speedometer. "Of course my speed right now is only fifty-five."

I stole some glances at him for a moment. "Try this, open your eyes and I'll explain a little about what I'm doing, that might help."

"I know what ye are doin', you are hurlin' this big car down the road at a verra fast speed."

I giggled. "Open your eyes buster, I'm going to show you." I started with the steering wheel, then the gas pedal, and the brake. I explained about putting it into drive. And how my foot was pushing down to give us forward momentum and my foot was at the ready to stop us. I actually couldn't believe I hadn't shown him any of this before. I slowed us down and sped back up. And the whole time he was watching me and not the road. Finally I said, "See, all that time and you forgot to have your eyes shut.

"I did, I may get used tae it after—" Just then we drove up and over a bridge and his eyes clamped shut again. I giggled, turned the music up, and continued to sing.

Parking the RV was not easy. But I accomplished it.

Cooking dinner in our tiny kitchen was ridiculous, but we laughed through it.

Sleeping in the tiny queen bed cramped tight against two walls was laughably not the worst bed we had ever slept in. Magnus said, "This car has a better bed than my whole century." And it was funny because it was true.

CHAPTER 46

The following morning we sunscreened our noses, packed our water bottles, stuffed some protein bars in our pockets — reminding me of going back in time — and met the boat to ride into the amusement park. All of this was new. Going somewhere like this. Crowds of people. Awesome, ridiculous Big Civilization Stuff, together.

Magnus stood firm and straight, protective, close. I watched the side of his face, his expression calm and uninterested, though his eyes flitted, checking the boat deck, watching the people, assessing the crowd, always hyper-aware of his surroundings, watching, thinking, learning. The crowds were awful. Pressing, jostling, pushing. Magnus found the whole thing unbelievable. And a lot too much to take in.

Once I hit the park and had the map in front of me, I couldn't think of a single thing he might enjoy. I went for the It's a Small World ride first. The line took an hour. I talked him through getting in the tiny boart and with a rush we were gestured in. I held his hand and we were off — Magnus's first amusement park ride.

It was dark and the small animatronic figures sang the song relentlessly. It was all glowing and overly happy and Magnus's face was very amused. He actually looked a little thrilled when the cart swung around to see the singing characters on the opposite side. When we stepped out I asked, "What did you think?"

"Twas extraordinary."

"For that you get Space Mountain next."

The line took two hours and fifteen minutes. There were many moments where I second guessed the wisdom of this whole exercise. But then with a rush we were pushed through to the seats. "Magnus, hold on to this bar, okay? Just go with it, it's going to be f—" and we were off. I clutched his hand. My style on roller coasters was a full blown giggle with squeals the entire time. It must have been infectious because Magnus said something like "whoa!" and then he was laughing, big belly laughs. The opposite of my high-pitched giggles but equally close to hysterical. His boomed from his chest and the sound followed us the whole way

We climbed from the cart at the end, Magnus's cheeks were flushed, his smile wide. "Did you keep your eyes open the whole time?"

"Nae, but twas a verra fine ride."

"We should have had lunch already but instead I want to introduce you to a Pineapple Whip and then..." A wave of nausea rose from my knees, through my core, and threatened to drop me to the ground. I clutched my stomach. "Ugh." I fanned myself.

"Are you alright, Kaitlyn?"

"No, I'm fine, I... Let's get something to eat and drink."

I led him through the pressing, jostling crowd to the closest food stand and bought two big Pineapple Whips for way too much money. Magnus ate his ravenously, standing beside a bench we were hoping someone would vacate so I could sit down because there was some very serious nausea happening now. I was hot. Sweaty. And about to throw up. I needed to lie down. Probably now.

I ate two mouthfuls of the dessert then said, "I think I need to go back to the RV."

"What do ye think tis?"

"I don't know, maybe morning sickness, a part of pregnancy?" I closed my eyes with a groan as a wave hit me again.

Magnus said, "Show me the map." I passed it to him and gave a faint point toward the area we were standing in. "We have tae get tae the dock?"

"Yeah."

"Okay, follow me." Magnus led me through the crowds across Disney World to the dock for our ferry to the campground. I was no help at all, I stared at the ground, the back of his legs, and trailed behind trying to keep my insides from coming up all over my outsides.

On the ferry I held on around his chest with my eyes closed. Sort of sleeping. In the RV we cranked the AC and I collapsed on the bed. "I'm sorry we left Disney World early."

"Twas enough."

I pulled my phone from my pocket and called Emma. "I'm in bed in the RV and I feel like barfing—"

She said, "Of course you have morning sickness." Like it was the most obvious thing in the world and not an, I don't know, consequence of dying because of the internal organ damage that being slung over the back of a horse caused a few weeks ago. That's where my mind went at first — total damage.

I slept and faded in and out of consciousness until later in the afternoon when I thought I might be able to stomach something. Then I rallied and ate a whole bag of Doritos. Half of the bag I dipped in nacho cheese sauce. While drinking a coke. I felt a lot better. We microwaved one of the dishes Zach sent for us, Fettuccini Alfredo, and then we built a fire as night came on and roasted marshmallows for dessert. It ended up being a really lovely night. And late, late we went for a walk and found an open dark space and we looked up at the stars, standing together under another night sky. My head on his shoulder, our hands clasped. "I love you Magnus."

"I love you too, Kaitlyn." He kissed the top of my head.

CHAPTER 47

The next morning we pulled out from our camping spot and headed south toward Miami and made it about three hours before I was so nauseous I had to pull us over into a truck stop. I cranked up the generator to run the AC, stumbled to the bed, and collapsed.

The bed shifted as Magnus sat on the edge of it. "I daena think ye can continue drivin'."

"Ugh." I said in answer.

I pulled my arm off my eyes to see him. "But we can't stay here. I have to drive I..." my voice trailed off. It was true but I couldn't imagine how it was going to happen. "We can wait until tonight and then I should be..."

Magnus smiled down at me. "You see your list on the wall?" He gestured toward the list I had been making since we got married. All the places I wanted to take my husband. It started with Disney World and NASA and the Keys, but then included the Natural History Museum, Washington DC, New Orleans, the route of Lewis and Clark, Mt Rushmore and Reno Nevada, the PCH and the Redwood trees. Yosemite National Park. "You got me tae the first one. You can check it off as ye do. We have our whole lives to see the list."

"I guess we do."

He smiled. "And from the looks of it we're goin' tae need our whole lives."

I fake cried, "That's why we can't go slow. We have tae do it all now," I pretended to pass out with my arms flung to the sides. "Who am I kidding? I can't do anything but whimper in this bed."

"In this wee bed," Magnus corrected and held out his hand. "Give me your phone." I fished my phone from my pocket and pushed the button for Quentin and passed it to him. Then I lay there doing exactly that, whimpering, while the rumbling voice of my husband handled whatever it was that needed handling. I couldn't imagine, or suspect, or even think what we were going to do. I could only sit and 'rest'.

Magnus disappeared a while later and reappeared with a bag of drinks and chips from the truck stop. I watched him for a moment as he stood in our tiny kitchen and opened Tupperware containers peeking inside and sniffing the contents. Then he ate something cold. I don't think I ever showed him how to use the microwave. It had never been necessary before.

"Do you need help with..." Who was I kidding? There wasn't any help I could give. I couldn't even speak in complete sentences.

A while later he climbed into bed and spooned up behind me. He smelled of sweat and heat and that scent he carried deep, spice and musk and ancient old. He wrapped me in it and a long time ago, maybe the moment I met him when I was huddled behind Hayley drunk out of my mind but sane enough to pay attention, I breathed him in, and I kept breathing — him, his thick arms around me, his broad chest pressed to my back, enveloped around. His voice rumbled in my ear. "Quentin is on his way." I nodded. It was going to be okay. He was taking care of me here, too.

Hours later there was a knock on our door. Magnus rose from the bed and I felt the shifting RV as he lumbered to the cab. A moment later Zach was standing there smiling. "How's it going there Katie?"

"Not good I'm..." Again with the not finishing sentences.

He joked, "You look great, like this whole vacation is totally agreeing with you."

Quentin appeared behind him. "So you've left the boss stranded at a truck stop, this is not following your itinerary."

"Keep joking and I'll throw up on your shoes."

They all laughed. Zach put a bag down in front of me. "Emma wanted me to make you Rice Krispy Treats, but I didn't have time so she made me buy these at the store. It's all that got her through morning sickness. She says to eat as many as you want. I bought you twenty." Then he and Magnus and Quentin discussed who would drive what, and they decided Zach would drive the Mustang home. Quentin would drive the RV. I would lay here on the bed and eat Rice Krispies Treats. Magnus would ride in the RV with me. And a few moments later we were headed up the highway home.

Magnus lay on the bed letting me curl up along his side opening Rice Krispies Treat packages and piling the empty packages on his chest because I could only take tiny bites and had to rest between them. "It's like that night at Balloch when you put the Hershey's kiss on my belly." I was beginning to feel a bit better, the treats were practically magic.

"Aye but twas too ordinary. This is an extraordinary moment."

I pulled my head up and looked down at him. "What? You think that was ordinary? A chocolate Kiss in an eighteenth century castle? And what is extraordinary about this? I've just ruined our vacation with my stupid body, which has a way of doing this, being a real jerk when I need to be capable."

"Kaitlyn we are in a truck moving verra fast down the road and we are in bed."

I chuckled. "Okay, that is a little extraordinary."

"You have taken me on a roller coaster and I was born in the seventeenth century."

"Yeah, that's definitely extraordinary."

"Kaitlyn Campbell is carrying my bairn and is about tae be the motherfucking matriarch of my branch of the family tree."

I giggled. "Now that's almost unbelievable." I took a big bite of a Rice Krispies Treat and ate with relish. "I'm starting to feel better."

The RV rolled and rocked as we traveled down the highway. "Good."

"So you've become a regular modern man, with the roller-coaster, making your own lunch, and that phone call earlier."

"Is that all it takes then? Much easier than I thought twas."

"So what now?"

"Now I train. Now we live. Now we wait for a bairn tae be born. I have been thinkin' on it while ye have been in bed. I will go first thing tae speak tae lady Mairead. Tis time. We want tae have some peace until she calls on me."

"You'll still have to be her warrior." I stated it as a fact not a question.

"Aye. That winna change, but the end result — I have a bairn. I will come home."

"Do you think you'll be here when the baby is born?"

"Aye. Nothing will keep me from ye, Kaitlyn." And we traveled home in our rocking shifting carriage, driven by our head of security. Headed into an uncertain future but in each other's arms in a certain present. Together.

CHAPTER 48

We were through Jacksonville when Quentin got a phone call. He held it to his ear while driving and seemed so intent on the conversation that I sat up to listen. Quentin said, "...she is?" Then he said, "Wait, let me talk to Boss."

He dropped the phone to his lap letting it slide off his leg to the ground. "Boss, that was Matthew, Lady Mairead is there."

Magnus stood and walked to the cab of the RV with his hands on the wall to steady himself. "What is she doin' there?"

"Matthew said she arrived up the boardwalk a few minutes ago. He told her she wasn't allowed on the property but she said she would wait for you. She's sitting on the back deck."

"Kaitlyn, call—"

"I'm already calling her." I pushed the button for Emma.

"Leave the house," I said as soon as she answered. "Grab Ben, leave, get to your car and go to — I don't know, like a coffee shop or something? We'll be home in..." I looked at the dashboard clock. "Forty minutes."

Her voice emitted, "What is it Kaitlyn? Okay, I'm headed to the front door, wait, I see — Lady Mairead is here?"

"She is, she's on the back deck. Please, please get out. We're almost back. Don't hang up, talk to me as you go so I don't freak out."

"I'm out the door, down the steps. Okay, three steps to the car. I'm there. I'm at the car. Wait — Ben is struggling. Shhhhhh. Shhh baby, get in the car seat." I could hear Ben screaming through the phone.

"Are you in the car? Are you...?"

All I could hear was the sound of Ben crying and I thought I might have a full blown hyperventilation attack right there. Finally she said, "Okay, I'm driving away. I'm out of the driveway. Okay, I'm done, I'm gone. Can you guys call Zach?"

Tears streamed down my face. "Quentin is already calling him. Where will you be?"

"Tell him I'm taking Ben to Michael's. To meet us there."

"I will, thank you Emma. Thank you for listening and getting yourself to safety and I'm so sorry, I'm so so sorry about this. Don't be scared. Magnus and I will figure out what to do."

I hung up, terrified.

Magnus sat on the edge of the passenger seat. I sat in the recliner in the back. Quentin drove. We were in silence except for the occasional question or vague statement. Mine: "What do you think she wants?"

Magnus's: "Are you carrying a weapon?" directed at Quentin.

Quentin's: "Should we drop Kaitlyn off at Michael's too?"

"Nae, she will need tae be at the house. I have a conversation tae have with Lady Mairead, Kaitlyn may need tae be present for it."

He turned to me. "But I need ye tae be verra quiet. Tae nae say a word, only tae me if I ask ye a question. She will want tae draw ye intae a negotiation, but I winna stand for it. I need ye tae follow my orders in this Kaitlyn."

I looked at him for a moment. "Yes. Of course. That makes sense. What did Zach say?"

Quentin said, "He's on his way to Michael's, but he said he would come if he was needed."

"Okay," I said and then we all drove in silence to the house.

Finally I said, "I thought she said she wasn't going to mess with us for six months?"

To which Magnus grunted. And began to strap his sword belt across his wide chest.

CHAPTER 49

hen we arrived at the house Quentin pulled the RV into the driveway. Magnus stalked through the RV to the back and slid his sword out from under the bed. I watched through the window as Quentin and Magnus stepped down to the pavement. When Quentin was performing his duties as a security guard he usually had a gun strapped to a shoulder holster, nestled near his ribs. But today he didn't. He hadn't been on official business, just driving, his gun was upstairs. He and Magnus stood outside of the RV and discussed quietly. I made out words as they murmured the strategies.

Magnus said, "...I'll go directly to the deck..."

Quentin said, "...I need to get to the cabinet for my piece..."

I sat there like I had been told. I was feeling better though the nausea had been replaced by cold icy fright, and I really wanted to go lie down again. But what? Something big was about to happen. The kind of thing I feared would change my life. And it wasn't just hyperbole, every conversation I ever had with Lady Mairead had changed my life drastically.

Magnus stuck his head in through the door. "Kaitlyn, we

need ye tae come up with us. I canna leave ye here." I clambered out of the RV and stood in between Magnus and Quentin and we ascended the stairs to our house.

The kitchen looked like Emma dropped everything to leave. There were dishes in the sink, a yogurt tub open with a spoon sticking out of the top. A chill crawled down my spine. Emma had been serving some yogurt and had emergency evacuated with her baby. I would need to pay her extra for that somehow.

Through the sliding door on the back deck was Lady Mairead, her stiff back sitting erect in one of my chairs. At my table. Under my goddamned umbrella. It was past dinner time but still hot as hell. I was glad she was in her wool garb. She was probably about to faint from the heat. Matthew, one of the new security hires we brought on while Magnus was home, was standing on the back deck with his arms folded. He was older, in his forties, and I felt like an ass giving him orders, and now I would need to give him combat pay for my mother-in-law. How long had he been standing there guarding her, over an hour? I'd have to double his pay.

As if she could hear us through the door Lady Mairead stood and smoothed out her skirt without turning. Magnus said, "Kaitlyn, follow Quentin please, to our room."

"Okay."

And Magnus walked straight for the back deck of our house. I watched him nod at Matthew, who relaxed a bit.

Then Magnus stood beside Lady Mairead and they began to talk. A breeze had picked up the curl of his hair and the edge of his kilt fabric fluttered a bit in a contrast to the stiff, unmoving, furiously solid body of my husband.

Quentin led me to the bedroom door using his body to block

the sight of me. He opened the door. "Stay here until he calls for you."

"You're going to be out there with him?"

"I'm going to stand right beside him. Don't worry Kaitlyn, we'll figure this out."

"Don't let him touch her, she might jump with him and then—"

"I won't. Just stay here."

CHAPTER 50

I sat on the edge of my bed watching Quentin's shoulder through the sliding glass door. This sucked. Boring, but yet my adrenaline was pumping. After a few minutes I walked around the bed and slid the door open a crack. I felt Quentin tense, but I wasn't coming out to the deck. I stood inside my room hidden behind Quentin, my ear pressed to the opening in the door.

Occasionally I made out small bits from Lady Mairead. "...You would attend me on the journey..."

Heat seeped in through the crack. It was blazing hot outside. I felt sorry for Magnus and Quentin and Matthew, all sweltering. I hoped Lady Mairead might pass out. A little heat exhaustion for the drama she was putting me through.

"...I am glad you are more amenable tae the idea..."

My husband's voice was indistinct, though I pressed closer trying to hear. He kept his voice measured and low. I glanced at the clock, it had been twenty minutes.

"...I do apologize for the treatment of your Kaitlyn..."

"...I am sure we can come tae a better agreement..."

Quentin whispered over his shoulder. "He's inviting her into the house."

I said, "shit." For lack of a better thing.

Magnus came to Quentin and said, "Have Kaitlyn call Zach, ask him tae come and bring food to serve. I have asked Lady Mairead to dinner."

I asked through the crack in the door, "What kind of food?"

Magnus said, "He may bring whatever he likes."

I lowered my voice. "No poison?"

"Tis nae the time for it." Then he was gone. I had kind of been joking but his voice didn't seem to be.

CHAPTER 51

I called Zach. He asked what kind of food he should bring, and I told him Magnus said to bring whatever he wanted. Then I sat on the bed and stared at the wall. I could hear Magnus's voice outside on the deck and then in the living room. I still couldn't hear well enough — blasted air conditioning hum. Their voices sounded like they were being pleasant. Then I heard Zach enter the house and the rustling of bags. I was super impressed he came considering how furious he must be for the fright Lady Mairead gave Emma. I would have to pay him extra too. Everybody would need a raise.

After so long it was getting quite dark outside and also inside because I didn't turn on lights, Magnus came into our room. He sat on the edge of our bed.

I swung my feet off the side and sat beside him. "How's it going?"

His pause was long. He looked at my face and brushed hair from my cheek and his fingertips traced down my jawline to my neck. "'Tis goin' as would be expected. I want tae kill her. And she would deserve it. But I am tryin' tae control my anger and come tae an agreement with your interest in mind. But och, she is shifty. She has agreed tae take the neckpiece from ye."

"What did you give up in return?"

He looked down at his hands. "I have given her my word that I will come when she calls."

My heart sank. "Today? Not today right? Not right now?"

"Not right now." He sighed. "She meant it tae be right now, but she has given me a reprieve because of the bairn ye be carryin'."

"Oh. Well that's good, right?"

"Aye." He rubbed his hand up and down on his thighs. "My question for you is would ye be able tae sit across from her at the dinner table considerin' your long history of troubles? I winna blame ye if you wanted tae sit here in the room but I would consider it a great favor if ye could come."

I put my hand on his. And rested my head on his shoulder. "Of course I'll come, what kind of food did Zach bring?"

"He has brought Mexican." He smiled a little. "He told me twill be verra spicy."

Magnus led me into the room and held a chair out for me at the table. He sat between me and Lady Mairead, allowing her to have the seat at the head of the table. Where she used to sit when she lived here. Everyone was quiet, tense, and nervous. Quentin stood against the wall behind me. Zach worked in the kitchen, completely quiet. He was wearing a dirk at his hip, one he used when he was sparring with Magnus. He kept glancing up at us occasionally. Awkwardly.

Lady Mairead said, "You are looking well Kaitlyn. You are carrying a bairn?"

I glanced at Magnus from the corner of my eye. He nodded. I answered, "Yes. I'm about a month along."

Her eyes twinkled, much like a look I had seen in her son's eyes, but where his were mischievous, her eyes were malevolent.

"I have said this before but it remains true, you have surprised me with your abilities, Kaitlyn Campbell. I believed ye to be capable, but you are devious in your art."

I didn't look at Magnus. I didn't need to. Answering that would throw me into a frenzy so better to remain quiet. I gulped down a small bite of burrito and stared at the chair back across from my seat.

"You made a deal with me, but now ye are carryin' a bairn, and I am tae let ye from your deal else I am made tae be a tyrant."

I chewed slowly. Wiped my mouth on my napkin.

Magnus said, "Lady Mairead, I expect ye tae refrain from insultin' Kaitlyn further."

She slowly watched me and then nodded. Her eyebrow arched carefully. "I see Magnus. You have curtailed her wild spirt. She asks your permission tae speak. She knows her place. You have handled it all very well."

Magnus growled.

"But then she has altered ye as well. You werena willing before tae speak tae me on these matters and here you are, pleading for my compassion. Bargaining and negotiating with me. I find ye both remarkably changed."

She ate a bite of her pinto beans with cheese. "I greatly admire a young woman who can accomplish taming a warrior such as yourself Magnus. Though I of course need you tae do battle for me, as we spoke of, daena let Kaitlyn make ye soft."

I glanced at Magnus.

It hadn't been that long ago that he argued I was making him soft. With vitamins. God, I hated my mother-in-law.

He stared straight ahead. Chewing. I wondered if anyone in

the history of the world had ever had such an awkward dinner party as this?

Lady Mairead ate another bite of beans, leaving the very spicy burrito sitting untouched. "I will need tae depart soon."

Magnus said, "You need tae remove the shackle first."

"True." She drew the syllable out long. "But I am nae amenable tae taking it off here. You are within a suitable distance tae cause me a great deal of harm. Your security guard is just there. Another on the back deck. As soon as the hold is off Kaitlyn's neck I will be in grave danger I would think."

"If you think I am lettin' ye take Kaitlyn anywhere else ye are gravely mistaken."

"You daena trust your mother, Magnus?" A chill ran up my spine.

"Nae."

"See you are verra confused on this matter. My word is absolutely tae be trusted. I have meant every single word I uttered here today."

Without knowing I was going to speak I said, "You told us you would leave us alone for six months, yet here you are, six weeks later."

"Ah." Her malevolent smile widened. "She does speak without permission. There's the Kaitlyn I remember. Kaitlyn, I have also brought you a peace offerin'. Tis over there against the wall."

A linen bag leaned in the corner of the living room stuffed bulging full of a lot of things. "I don't believe it does any harm tae come visit my family. My daughter is about tae give me another grandchild. I have come bearing gifts. I wasna expecting a renegotiation of our deal, yet here we are. Is your word tae be trusted Magnus?" She paused, staring at his stoic face, his jaw clenching and unclenching. I watched from my periphery. I swear to god the gold plating around my neck felt tighter.

She continued, "I believe ye mean tae be. You have a bairn on the way. You have come tae me with a vow. I trust ye tae do what ye have promised, so I will take the shackle off of Kaitlyn's neck. I will do it though, without ye shadowing over me."

She pulled the napkin from her lap and put it beside her plate. "Kaitlyn, we will walk to the end of the deck."

I glanced at Magnus, he nodded stiffly. I stood from my chair. He gestured to Quentin who stepped behind me. I glanced at Zach who was watching from the kitchen.

Magnus said, "If I'm not tae come with ye, I would like Zach tae attend Kaitlyn tae the beach."

"Ah, Chef Zach are ye a guard of our castle now?"

He came around the kitchen island. "I know my way around a knife."

Lady Mairead laughed appreciatively. She stood. "Follow me, Kaitlyn."

I walked behind her. My hands were shaking and I felt like crumpling into a ball. But instead I had to walk out into the night following someone who wished me a great deal of harm. Magnus had warned me about the danger of being married to him but though I had tried to imagine it I couldn't have known this. I wasn't sure I had the strength this required. I wished I had my knife, but I lost it back in 1702 and hadn't come up with a reason to buy another.

We walked single file to the end of the deck. Our footsteps thudding down the planks. It was dark yet still sweltering hot. Very hot. Sweat bloomed from my skin. I took a bit of joy that Lady Mairead must be desperately hot. Of course that would make her pretty pissy too.

Zach walked behind me. Magnus and Quentin remained on the back deck beside the sliding glass doors. I watched them gesture and make eye contact exchanging signals about a plan. A plan that probably involved the gun Quentin had strapped to his chest, but now they were behind me and I was blocking Lady Mairead so I had little hope that it would work. Plus the last thing Quentin needed to do was shoot someone on our deck. He would be in so much trouble.

At the end of the deck Lady Mairead descended the steps to the sand and led me across the dune in the dark. To the right were three stakes with caution tape strung around a sea turtle nest. I hadn't realized it was there. The turtle must have laid the eggs while we were on our vacation.

The sea turtles were protected. Like I was being protected. I just had to do this one thing — follow Lady Mairead out to the beach and allow her to take the shackle off my neck. Then I could go back to being with Magnus. Waiting for the baby.

What had he promised her?

Lady Mairead pulled to a stop. She arched her brow and commanded. "Step forward, Kaitlyn."

I raised my chin while she adjusted the hair off my shoulders.

She said, "Despite your suspicions, Magnus needs my protection in the coming months. Just as I need his. I really do have his best interests at heart."

Her hands went around my throat and peeled the gold leaf from my neck. It felt satisfying, like pulling Elmer's glue off my skin, but also sent chills down my back. The proximity of her breath, the sweat rolling down my skin, the darkness all around. I knew Zach was just behind me, but I had no idea where —

I asked, "What deal did he make?"

She stepped back with the neck piece in her hand, now returned to a small circular piece much like a bracelet. "You will need tae ask Magnus for the details. They daena include ye so I winna inform ye of them." She reached into her sporran and retrieved the time vessel. "You may return to the house now. It was a pleasure seeing you again Chef Zach, give my regards tae Emma."

I walked across the dunes fast, hearing my mother-in-law muttering numbers behind me.

Zach pulled in and jogged behind me, close. My feet hit the steps as the storm began to churn, wind and electricity and a roaring noise. I jogged down the boardwalk with Magnus jogging toward me. We met in the middle and I fell into his arms crying.

He held me fast. "Tis okay now Kaitlyn, tis over." He faced the beach, but I couldn't watch. I held my head in his shirt waiting for someone to give me the all clear. To tell me she was finally gone.

We got into the living room and Zach started it, "What the fuck was that? That was seriously fucked up! Did you see me though? I was eyeing her, had my hand on my sword. I would have done it too if I needed to, but man, that was—"

Magnus said, "Chef Zach, you were a true warrior standing out there in the sand. I was sure ye would rescue Kaitlyn if twas necessary."

Zach said, "I have to go call Emma. We're cool now, right? She can come home?"

Magnus said, "Aye, she can come home."

CHAPTER 52

*M*agnus wouldn't tell me about the deal.

When I asked him that night in bed, he said, "You ken about it if ye think on it. Tis nae different really from the deal we had afore..." His hand stroked up and down on my arm. "Tis nae that I want tae keep it from ye, but I daena want tae speak it."

"I need to hear it."

"The physician said the bairn will be hearin' me."

"Oh. I guess so... I mean kind of..."

"Inna that what the physician said?"

"Yes, that the baby can hear your voice."

"I dinna ken the bairn would be listenin'. I daena want tae frighten him."

I snuggled into his arms.

"I would like tae spend this respite with ye and nae discuss it more. I daena want it tae be all we think on. I am protectin' ye. I am keepin' the bairn safe. I need it tae be enough."

Our room was dark except for the moon-glow outside casting some light across our marital bed. I was held in his arms. My throat wasn't tight. Not from the outside anyway though I felt a little lump from the tears that wanted to build there. I wanted to force Magnus to tell me all the details of his discussion with Lady Mairead, but he couldn't speak it. And he had told me that talking after a battle was important and here he was not doing it.

I had to accept that he couldn't do it. He wasn't hiding it from me. I knew what it was. Really. He had traded his life for mine. And I didn't know what that meant, but I had the answer in that he didn't want to worry me with it. And he didn't want to worry over it. He wanted to hold me. Spend all the time he could with me.

And how could I argue with that?

I couldn't.

So I held him. And he held me. After a few long moments and tender caresses, I asked, "Did she give you a time, any specifics on when?"

"The moon before Yule."

I took a deep breath. "So like, just before Christmas, in December?"

The word, Aye, rumbled up from his chest.

"And the baby's due date is the end of March."

"I will do everythin' in my power tae get back tae ye in time."

"Okay." I nodded on his chest. "Okay," I said again as if repeating it made it certain.

CHAPTER 53

*T*here wasn't much that changed about Florida in the fall. A tiny bit cooler perhaps.

Magnus and I knew our baby was a little boy. I felt like Magnus would want to know before he left so we had an ultrasound. Just in case he missed the birth. Though we still weren't talking about the possibility of him missing it. We weren't talking about any of it. It was still two months away when he would leave.

Two months.

He spent every day in training. Quentin and I designed a plan based on a Men's Health magazine article about Chris Hemsworth's Thor workout. We figured that would be about right. Then we realized that Quentin and I didn't know jack-shit about training a time-journeyer for a future-battle, so I hired him a personal trainer. Someone who specialized in MMA and had a history of training with a sword.

Zach bulked him up. Magnus was on a special diet which pissed him off greatly. He managed to sweet talk his way into a bowl of ice cream every night though. And me too. I was bulking up just in different places. My stomach rounded in the front and Magnus couldn't keep his hands off of it.

～

We set the alarm so he could go train, but first Magnus scrunched down in the bed until he was eye level to my tummy. He spoke to the baby. "Good mornin' bairn. You are well this morn?" He kissed my belly and right then there was a flutter, a tiny bit of movement in my lower pelvis, small but unmistakable.

My eyes widened. "Did you feel that? Right here, oh my god, Magnus, the baby was moving right here." I pulled his hand to my stomach below my bellybutton. "Wait, wait right there. It was the most amazing thing — just hold your hand like that."

We both sat quietly, waiting. Nothing more happened. "Maybe talk to it again."

Magnus whispered, his lips brushing against my belly, sending sweet sexy shivers up my skin, "Gum bi thu, a naoinein bhig, fallain, sona air feadh—"

The flutter happened again.

Magnus looked up at me with a wide smile and I burst into happy tears. "Wait, hold that, hold it right there, okay?" I wiggled up to the side table, grabbed my phone, hit the video camera button, and pointed it down at my belly with my husband's face pressed to my skin. I hit 'record'. "Magnus, talk to the baby again."

"Gum bi thu, a naoinein bhig, fa—" He smiled again. "He is movin'."

"I can feel it. Isn't it the most amazing thing in the world?"

"Tis a miracle, Kaitlyn." He planted a big kiss on my belly and then wriggled up my body to kiss me on the lips. I kept the camera rolling and when Magnus noticed it in my hand he laughed, our mouths pressed together.

"One selfie." I held the camera up, pointed at our faces, his lips pressed to mine with a laugh between them. Happy tears sparkling on my cheeks.

I snapped the photo.

It was a moment I never ever wanted to forget.

CHAPTER 54

*M*agnus went to the gym to meet his trainer. He would be gone for hours.

Emma and I spent way too long at Target buying Halloween decorations, candy, and costume parts. Everything we considered from one aspect — would Magnus think this is amazing? If the answer was yes, we tossed it in our cart. There was no plan to our decorating. Our carts looked like a Halloween Pop-up Superstore exploded in them. Because yes, we had to get a second cart. I had no idea if there would be any trick-or-treaters in our part of the neighborhood but I bought a massive amount of candy because again, Magnus would think it was amazing.

Halloween was, now that I thought about it through his filter, almost as amazing as the fireworks at Fourth of July. And they had given him such a thrill I wondered if he would be able to sleep that night.

And soon would be Thanksgiving, imagine Magnus at a feast like that?

Imagine Christmas — I stopped myself remembering he wouldn't be there. Where would he be? Or when?

Emma and I, with Baby Ben, drove over to Hayley's office to talk her into going to a restaurant with us for lunch. I walked in with a terrifying mask on to scare the shit out of her and she said, "Hi Katie, what are you up to today?"

We all devolved into laughter.

"Coming to get you for lunch."

Hayley said, "I can't! Look at all the work I have!" She collapsed on her desk and pretend to cry for a moment. Then she stood up. "I'm kidding, I can always take a day. Where to? I suppose it has to be somewhere that accepts babies?"

I rolled my eyes. "Jesus Christ Aunt Hayley, all restaurants accept babies."

"But should they? I mean I'm only mentioning this because I'm Ben's aunt, but he wears diapers."

Emma said, "How would you know, you've never changed them?"

"And I won't. Not for my nephew and not for your baby, Katie. No matter how much you beg. It's not my style." She grabbed her purse and keys, locked the front door, and we made our way to a little restaurant just off Centre Street.

Between the three of us we knew basically the entire staff. We got a great table in the corner. Hayley ordered a grown up drink, Emma went with water because she was nursing, I asked for a coke because I needed the sugar-carbonation-cold ice thing. The menus were delivered and the waitress took our order. But the problem was I was starting to not feel so good. Kind of overly hot. Kind of not right. I watched Emma and Hayley talk about the brothers, one of their favorite subjects. They commiserated about behaviors like the weird noise Zach and Michael made while brushing their teeth and—

I clutched my stomach. "Ugh."

Emma looked at me quizzically. "You look positively green."

"Your conversation is pretty gross."

Our food was delivered. My head was spinning.

And suddenly it felt a lot like I was having a period cramp. Like a doozy. I moaned and put my head on my hand. Then down on the table. "I really don't feel good."

Hayley held my hand stroking the back of it. "Maybe you just need to eat?"

Emma asked, "Where is it?" She looked under the table to see my hand clutching at my lower pelvis. "Does it feel like your period?"

I nodded on my arm. My eyes closed, sweat blooming on my face. "Ugh." I groaned

Hayley asked, "Is it the baby?"

Emma said, "I don't know." She came to my side. "Can you stand up?" Her arm went around my back and she helped to heave me to my feet and that's when they saw it — the blood on the back of my dress. I didn't need to see it, I knew from their voices.

"Oh honey," Hayley said, "we need to get you to—"

I dropped my head back on my arm on the table. "I can't..."

Next thing I heard Emma's voice saying into the phone, "Yes, I need an ambulance at the Patio on third street. Yes."

Hayley was explaining to our waitress. A crowd was gathering. And all I could do was lay there while my body mutinied against me. With my baby's life in the balance.

When the ambulance arrived Hayley was clutching my hand. She was not good with blood so I was pretty impressed she was still with me. She said, "First of all these hunky first responders — not that you care, your husband is way way hotter — are going to put you up on the stretcher." I was lifted. "There we go, honey —

you got this?" I shook my head. "You got this. You're going to go to the hospital and they'll get it sorted out."

"Is the baby going to..." I couldn't finish.

"Have you ever not done what you set out to do, sweetie? Never, I don't think you're going to stop now. You're my personal hero and this is just another thing you have to do." She stroked the hair off my head and followed the stretcher as the men wheeled me cramping and moaning to the back of the ambulance.

"Did Emma call Zach? Tell him to go get Magnus."

Hayley looked across the room at Emma. "She's on the phone now. She's getting him."

I moaned again. "Owie owie owie. It hurts."

As my stretcher slid into the back of the ambulance, I said, "He's afraid of hospitals will you help him get to me?"

"Of course, honey, we'll be there in a hot minute."

And then the ambulance doors shut closed behind me and an oxygen mask was placed over my face.

CHAPTER 55

The blinds were pulled on the room, a big heavy hotel-room-style curtain was pulled over the window. Though it was afternoon outside, my room was thrown into a melancholy, super sad, gray, dusk-like darkness. The door opened softly and —

Magnus.

"Kaitlyn."

Tears were damp on my cheeks, my body curled into the fetal position. I had been facing the door though, waiting.

"I'm sorry. I'm so so sorry." Tears rolled down my cheeks pooling onto the peaks and valleys of my fists. "I'm sorry." I repeated as he pulled a chair up to the bed.

"Shhhhh." He stroked my hair back from my cheek and kissed my damp knuckle and then perched on the edge of his chair his wide shoulders spread across me. He wrapped an arm around my head, the other arm around my thighs, and pulled my body toward him nuzzling his head into the side of my belly. His cheeks were wet. He pressed his face to my bed gown and held on. Like he would never let go.

"I miss him." I sobbed and he held on tighter.

His head burrowed into my side. "Och aye, mo reul-iuil."

"I tried, I didn't mean to. I wanted him so badly and I—"

His hand released my thighs and he held the back of my head cuddling me nose to wet crying nose. "I ken ye tried Kaitlyn, he just wasna ready for this world."

I sniffled. "I feel so empty. So broken. I wanted to have your baby. And I don't know why I—"

"You are perfect, mo reul-iuil — if there is blame tis mine tae bear." He stroked a hand down my hair around my shoulder and down my back and then he snuggled into my stomach again.

I focused on my fingers. "My body just stopped. And I must be broken that I couldn't do it."

"I have brought this on ye." His voice came up from the folds of fabric on my puffy stomach. "If you are broken, tis my doin'. I have brought nothin' but despair and—"

I touched the back of his hair and wrapped one of the curls around my fingers. "You haven't broken me, you filled me with so much. My heart, my life, my body. It's me that couldn't do this... and I think — I'm just so sad."

"I ken ye are, mo reul-iuil. I am too." His arms went back around me wrapping my torso around his head. He held me still and quiet. Both of us with silent tears rolling down our faces. "You ken I love ye?"

I nodded.

"Where do ye ken it?" His voice was a whisper.

"I know it here." I touched my ear. "Because you tell it to me."

"Tha gaol agam org, I love ye, mo reul-iuil, is ann leatsa abhios mo chridhe gubrath. My heart is yours." He rubbed his wet cheeks on my bed gown. "Where else do ye ken it?"

"I used to know it here." I patted my stomach with more tears rolling down my face.

He kissed my hand and buried his face there.

"Now it feels so empty."

His voice came from his chest like a rumble. "I miss the wee braw lad."

"Me too."

"How else do ye ken?"

"That you love me?" I put my damp hand over my breast. "I know it here."

"Och aye, I feel it there as well."

"And here." A sad-laugh escaped me as I patted between my legs.

He smiled a bit. "I once said I would live there if I could, and I meant it."

"And here." I rubbed my wrists. "I can feel the bindings that tied us together."

"'Tis like a vibration on my skin." He raised his wrist near me and I clutched his hand and kissed that place on his wrist where his pulse was the strongest. "Anywhere else?" he asked quietly

"Everywhere."

"You ken it in your marrow, Kaitlyn? Will ye remember how much I have loved ye when I am gone?"

I sobbed as the certainty that he was leaving hit me. I forced out the painful words. "I will."

He wrapped his hands around mine and then he stroked down my cheek and rubbed his strong hand down my whole side and then he went back to clutching my hands, his face drawn near. "And ye ken I have tae go?"

I nodded.

"I daena want tae. You will hold this in your heart?"

"I do. I know you don't want to go, but you have to."

"And I canna take ye. I daena ken what the future holds and..."

"I know. You have to go without me." I sniffled, trying to hold my tears in. There would be time enough for crying when he was gone.

He pressed his forehead to our hands. "Thank you, mo reul-iuil." He kissed my fingers. "I daena want tae leave ye here, but I canna leave when you are home."

My bottom lip trembled. "I get that. It would be really hard to watch you go."

He raised up still clutching my hands. "And I daena ken if the danger to you has passed. I canna let you be used against me. I think twould be best if ye removed from the house."

I nodded with a sob. "What if I moved to the new apartment building? It's a few miles away. Would that be hidden enough?"

"I think so. But keep Quentin close."

"Do you remember how to get there?"

The grim gray darkness was all around us as he whispered, "I do."

I concentrated on the angle of his thumb wrapped around my hands. "Then that's where I'll go."

"I will always be comin' home tae ye. Always."

"I know." I tightened my hold on his hands and drew them in and kissed the end of his thumb. I stared into his eyes for a long, long moment — *I love you* — he closed his eyes, his brow drawn, his pain evident. I watched his face memorizing the forms — the angles of his nose and the strong line of his jaw. My bottom lip trembled as I ran my fingers down his temple, the soft edge at the corner of his eyes. The wrinkle that would come once he ever smiled again.

If...

I traced the curve of his ear, the scar that was now familiar. He was so much a part of me being without him would — "Can you hold me for a little longer before you go?"

"Och aye, mo reul-iuil, I will stay til the morn," and he

climbed onto the bed and wrapped around my body and held me
like it might be our last time.

THANK YOU

*T*his is still not the true end of Magnus and Kaitlyn. There are more chapters in their story. If you need help getting through the pause before the next book, there is a FB group here: Kaitlyn and the Highlander Group

Thank you for sticking with this tale. I wanted to write about a grand love, a marriage, that lasts for a long long time. I also wanted to write an adventure. And I wanted to make it fun. The world is full of entertainment and I appreciate that you chose to spend even more time with Magnus and Kaitlyn. I just love them and wish them the best life, I will do my best to write it well.

As you know, reviews are the best social proof a book can have, and I would greatly appreciate your review on these books.

Kaitlyn and the Highlander (Book 1)
Time and Space Between Us (Book 2)
Warrior of My Own (Book 3)
Begin Where We Are (Book 4)
A Missing Entanglement (short story 4.5)

Entangled with You (Book 5)
to be named soon... (Book 6)
(book 7?)

SOME THOUGHTS AND RESEARCH...

Some **Scottish and Gaelic words** that appear within the books:

Turadh - a break in the clouds between showers

Solasta - luminous shining (possible nickname)

Splang - flash, spark, sparkle

Dreich - dull and miserable weather

Mo reul-iuil - my North Star (nickname)

Tha thu a 'fàileadh mar ghaoith - you have the scent of a breeze.

Osna - a sigh

Rionnag - star

Sollier - bright

Ghrian - the sun

Mo ghradh - my own love

Tha thu breagha - you are beautiful

Mo chroi - my heart

Corrachag-cagail - dancing and flickering ember flames

Mo reul-iuil, is ann leatsa abhios mo chridhe gubrath - My North Star, my heart belongs to you forever

Dinna ken - didn't know

Tha I fuar an-diugh. (*It is cold today)

Gum bi thu, a naoinein bhig, fallain, ionraic, sona air feadh do bheatha gu le\ir — *May you, little baby, be healthy, upright and happy throughout your whole life*

～

Characters:

Kaitlyn Maude Sheffield
Magnus Archibald Caelhin Campbell
Lady Mairead (Campbell) Delapointe
John Sheffield (Kaitlyn's father)
Paige Sheffield (Kaitlyn's Mother)
James Cook
Quentin Peters
Zach Greene
Emma Garcia
Michael Greene
Hayley Sherman
The Earl of Breadalbane
Uncle Archibald (Baldie) Campbell

～

Locations:

Fernandina Beach on Amelia Island, Florida, 2017-2018

Magnus's castle - Balloch. Built in 1552. In early 1800s it was rebuilt as Taymouth Castle. Situated on the south bank of the River Tay, in the heart of the Grampian Mountains

ACKNOWLEDGMENTS

My Facebook page was kicking it for a while there. My friends and family weighed in on questions like, "What should my Highlander's name be?" And "What would James call the Scottish National Football Team?" And "Which restaurant in downtown Fernandina Beach should I destroy?" Then we took the conversation over to Kaitlyn and the Highlander, my FB group and they answered even more questions for me, like "Were kilts too cold for a Scottish winter?"

There are too many people to thank, but thank you to Nipuna Devi Dasi for her input on using rendered goose fat on clothes for warmth (needed in book three!)

And to the friends who weighed in on how much our Magnus would know about menstruation, thank you for your thoughts. Ann McKeown for so much great information, Denise Sumpter for assuring me that Magnus wouldn't be a virgin on his wedding night. Anna Yori for the history of periods article, Anne LeMar for her ideas, and Kristen Schoenmann De Haan for her input.

And thank you to David Sutton for weighing in on many

things from Scottish customs (housing in the eighteenth century really helped with book 3) to what Magnus would find entrancing in the family planning aisle of the drug store.

And to David Sutton, Kristen Schoenmann De Haan, Heather Hawkes, Nipuna Devi Dasi, Catie Lane, Stacey Hirt, Amie Conrad, and Dru Mitchell for adding to Kaitlyn's list of places she wants to take Magnus. The list is so long there will need to be many more books.

There are so many other reasons to thank so many people. I am grateful for all the loving guidance I received. And to Heather Hawkes, Kristen Schoenmann De Haan, and David Sutton for being fabulous beta readers, you guys are awesome.

Thank you to Kevin Dowdee for being my support, my guidance, and my inspiration for these stories. I appreciate you so much. And thank you for revisiting Scotland with me on our honeymoon. That was awesome.

Thank you to my kids, Ean, Gwynnie, Fiona, and Isobel, for listening to me go on and on about these characters and accepting them as real parts of our lives. When I asked, "Guess what Magnus's favorite flavor of ice cream is?" They answered, "Vanilla," without blinking an eye. Also, when I asked, "What is Magnus's favorite band?" They answered, "Foo Fighters." (necessary in book 2) So yeah, thank you for thinking of my book characters like a part of our family.

ALSO BY DIANA KNIGHTLEY

Can he see to the depths of her mystery before it's too late?

The oceans cover everything, the apocalypse is behind them. Before them is just water, leveling. And in the middle — they find each other.

On a desolate, military-run Outpost, Beckett is waiting.

Then Luna bumps her paddleboard up to the glass windows and disrupts his everything.

And soon Beckett has something and someone to live for. Finally. But their survival depends on discovering what she's hiding, what she won't tell him.

Because some things are too painful to speak out loud.

With the clock ticking, the water rising, and the storms growing, hang on while Beckett and Luna desperately try to rescue each other in Leveling, *the epic, steamy, and suspenseful first book of the trilogy, Luna's Story:*

Leveling: Book One of Luna's Story

Under: Book Two of Luna's Story

Deep: Book Three of Luna's Story

ABOUT ME, DIANA KNIGHTLEY

I live in Los Angeles where we have a lot of apocalyptic tendencies that we overcome by wishful thinking. Also great beaches. I maintain a lot of people in a small house, too many pets, and a to-do list that is longer than it should be, because my main rule is: Art, play, fun, before housework. My kids say I am a cool mom because I try to be kind. I'm married to a guy who is like a water god, he surfs, he paddle boards, he built a boat. I'm a huge fan.

I write about heroes and tragedies and magical whisperings and always forever happily ever afters. I love that scene where the two are desperate to be together but can't because of war or apocalyptic-stuff or (scientifically sound!) time-jumping and he is begging the universe with a plead in his heart and she is distraught (yet still strong) and somehow, through kisses and steamy more and hope and heaps and piles of true love, they manage to come out on the other side.

I like a man in a kilt, especially if he looks like a Hemsworth, doesn't matter, Liam or Chris.

My couples so far include Beckett and Luna (from the trilogy, Luna's Story). Who battle their fear to find each other during an apocalypse of rising waters. And, coming soon, Magnus and Kaitlyn (from the series Kaitlyn and the Highlander). Who find themselves traveling through time and space to be together.

I write under two pen names, this one here, Diana Knightley, and another one, H. D. Knightley, where I write books for Young

Adults. (They are still romantic and fun and sometimes steamy though, because love is grand at any age.)

DianaKnightley.com
Diana@dianaknightley.com

ALSO BY H. D. KNIGHTLEY (MY YA PEN NAME)

  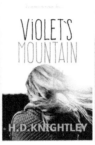 

Bright (Book One of The Estelle Series)

Beyond (Book Two of The Estelle Series)

Belief (Book Three of The Estelle Series)

Fly; The Light Princess Retold

Violet's Mountain

Sid and Teddy

Printed in Great Britain
by Amazon